REVIEWS

"Read the whole book in one night. Couldn't put it down. Realistic – I've seen many young people with such promise become Samantha, but I didn't really expect what happened to her. Got mad at John in the hospital bathroom … who could be that smart and that stupid. Couldn't figure out who the killer is. An award-winning story."

—Richard Winters, former Mayor,
Liberty, New York

"The unusual introduction all came together at the end. Samantha's father should have helped her in spite of tough love … that's what families are for. Read the whole thing twice. On the plane coming back from Tahoe, couldn't put my phone down even though it was a pain trying to find the pages where I left off. Then I read it again on my Kindle as soon as I got home."

—Lynn Lippelt, administrator,
Sullivan County Infirmary, New York

"OMG … Samantha … I know her in my heart. It feels like I've seen that courtroom. I just keep reading and reading and reading, putting all the clues together. I cried myself to sleep for Samantha last night."

—Megan Andrews, barn wedding catering,
Woodbourne, New York

"I know these people. I know these places. This is what our life is really like. I read lots of romance novels and Babies for Sale ranks right up there with them. I kept fitting everything together. I had to keep reading to find out what happened. This book kept me up at night."

—Linda Bowers, horse owner, housewife,
Hurleyville, New York

Photo by Megan Andrews

EDWARD DAVID LAGARDE, Ph.D, author, a retired executive, who has written on succession planning, is embarking on a series of social injustice murder mysteries. He spent seven years volunteering as a Court Appointed Special Advocate working with children and their families.

KAREN WORSTELL LAGARDE, corroborative author, was a former financial advice columnist and corporate publication editor. She volunteered for years by interacting with social services agency representatives to support young qualified people to receive benefits they deserved.

JUSTICE SERVED

Babies for Sale

EDWARD DAVID LAGARDE
KAREN WORSTELL LAGARDE

Epigraph Books
Rhinebeck, New York

Justice Served: Babies for Sale © 2017 by Edward David Lagarde and Karen Worstell Lagarde

Paperback ISBN: 978-1-944037-80-2
Hardcover ISBN: 978-1-944037-81-9
eBook ISBN: 978-1-944037-82-6
Library of Congress Control Number: 2017958428

Epigraph Books
22 East Market Street, Suite 304
Rhinebeck, New York 12572
(845) 876-4861
www.epigraphps.com

DEDICATION

To all the Samantha's of the world who make us ask, "Why?"
"Why don't you follow the rules?" "Why don't you take advantage of at least some of life's opportunities?" We love you. We care about you. We want you to succeed. You won't help yourself AND you won't let us help you. That troubles us. We can only hope that in time you will have the Justice Served that belongs to you.

—Edward David Lagarde
—Karen Worstell Lagarde

ACKNOWLEDGMENT

A special thanks to Sullivan County New York CASA, which provides screened trained and supervised volunteers who are appointed by the Family Court Judge to speak up for the needs of abused, neglected and abandoned children. The volunteers advocate for the best interests of the children, one child at a time, and are dedicated to reducing the amount of time a child spends in temporary foster care, seeking a safe, permanent and nurturing home for every child.

PROLOGUE

———◆———

"**G**OOD MORNING," was the lilting, singsong greeting by the aide as she drew open the drapes to darkness.

"Uuuuuuuuuuu."

"Time to wake up."

"Are you crazy? Not even a streak in the sky!"

"Come on, sunshine."

"There isn't any sunshine and I'm not sunshine. The only way I would be sunshine is if you had some valium in your pocket. I know I can have it; you just won't give it to me."

"Now, Now. Let me get you ready. There is going to be a beautiful, beautiful morning. And you and I are going to go out and see it."

"Uuuuuuu. Don't you ever get tired of being a phony … all bright and sparkly."

"No, no, no. Come on now, chicky. Let me brush your hair for you."

"You shouldn't get too close to me with that brush or *you* will be the chicky … with a broken neck."

"Shh, shh. See … your hair is still beautiful and curly.

Everybody is going to see how lovely you look. Time to go. We don't want to miss the sunrise."

"Ok, ok. Anything to get you off my back."

The aide kept clucking as she wheeled the wizened woman out in the wheel chair.

"This morning the cafeteria is going to have your favorite Scottish tea. And we'll have a little milk in it with sugar."

"And you'll spill the tea in my lap while you blab with everybody."

"I'm not gonna do that. Be nice. Now, move your legs so we can get your wheelchair out. 'Hello, Joseph.' Look at these new cafeteria doors, dearie ... they open right up for us. And the van is here waiting to go to Perkins Tower at the Bear Mountain State Park. It's a place where you can see for miles and miles and miles. So wonderful."

Her gushing was met with hostile silence.

The aide carefully guided the wheelchair onto the van lift, climbed into the passenger seat and solicitously looked back to keep an eye on her ward to whom she was devoted despite the caustic personality. As they went North on Route 9W and wound through the wooded park, the older woman did not hold back her sarcastic complaints.

Upon arrival, the aide pushed the wheelchair towards the lookout point.

"Oh, look at the neon pink peeping over the horizon. The sun is coming up. See, I told you it would be beautiful."

"You stupid selfish biddy. How could I see from here? Take me further so I can have a look. Don't you have any sense. Come on, get going!"

"Wow, it's really steep. We have to be careful now, dearie."

"Yeah, well, you're strong. Look at the arms on you. You look like a construction worker."

"I know, I know. Hmmm; I see a good tree on that flat rock. I can hang onto the branch and your wheelchair at the same time, so we'll be all right."

As the aide pushed the wheelchair towards the edge of the mountainside there was a sudden loud sharp clap … behind them … smoke spewed from a crevice. She snapped her head around, and saw a boulder starting to move, as though it were waking up. It was going to roll. She grabbed an overhanging branch and desperately tightened her other hand on the wheelchair. But it was too heavy; her ward slipped; the ground started to crumble and gave way.

"Help! Help! Help me you stupid bitch. You're letting me ……… Help! Help! Help!!!"

The aide began sobbing with the futility of her incapacity, a grimace on her face because she didn't save her ward. The only thing she could do was hold onto the branch for dear life.

As the wheelchair plunged off the edge of the cliff it tumbled over and over; legs flopped out; arms grasped for twigs, stones and the air; the chair rolled and smashed her bones against the rock outcropping; the boulders flew around banging and bruising; her screams for help were inhuman.

And then it was over.

There was nothing left but rubble.

But, no, there's a foot sticking out. And is that an arm? Is the finger on her hand moving or is that the smoke and dust rising like ashes?

"Waaaa. Waaaa." The screeching crescendoed as turkey vultures flocked above.

"Waaaa. Waa, waa, waaaaa!!!" Circling, circling and circling. Seeking the next meal.

Was that a whimper? A sob? A cry for forgiveness from our God in Heaven?

CHAPTER 1

———◆———

1950 - SAMANTHA LYNN JONES entered the world on a cold winter morning in November.

At 5:00 a.m. Rose awoke suddenly with a sharp pain in her stomach. She reached down and felt the completely soaked bed and called out to her husband.

"Get my suitcase; my water broke." Henry, barely awake and feeling the effects of a wet bed, got up and stumbled around in the dark trying to find the closet that contained his wife's suitcase.

After floundering for a few minutes, he called out,

"I can't find it."

"It's in the front closet in the girls' room."

"Oh, man. Why didn't I remember that."

Finally, he located the suitcase and headed for the front door.

"I'm getting the truck right now, Rosie. Just hang on."

"Okay."

He jumped down the front stairs and ran to the garage.

"I just hope the truck will start."

As he put the key into the ignition and turned it, the engine did not turn over.

"Damn! I can't believe this."

Rose called out in the distance, "The baby is coming!"

Henry mumbled to himself – "I know, I know; please God, let this truck start!"

After pumping the gas pedal several times more, the engine started, he put the truck in drive and headed for the house. Rose was standing at the bottom of the front stairs holding their daughter Virginia's hand.

As he pulled up, she yelled at him,

"Henry, this baby is demanding to get out. Hope there's not too much traffic so you can drive fast ... unless you want to play doctor and deliver it yourself ..." Rose said with a wry smile.

Henry winced and maneuvered the winding, rough road to Harris Hospital. Rose felt every bump.

"Oh my God, why can't they do the repairs more often. I don't know which is worse, slowing down to miss a few bumps or toughing it out so we can go faster."

Henry just smiled and did his best. It took 25 minutes to reach the emergency room ... a new record time. He pulled the truck into the closest parking space, jumped out and ran for the rotating door. As he reached it he realized Rose was not with him. He turned around and loped back to the truck as fast as his big frame would allow. She was sitting with her arms crossed, holding her belly as if to keep the baby from popping out.

"Forget something?"

Henry bowed his head, turned off the truck, and helped his Rose get out. They held hands as they entered the hospital.

CHAPTER 2

———◆———

As SOON AS HENRY SAW THE NURSE he said, "My wife is going to have a baby," and repeated it several times.

The nurse just nodded and proceeded to take information from Rose. She put on the wrist band and double-checked the name. Then she instructed the orderly to take her to maternity on the 5th floor. He wheeled the expectant mother down the corridor while the nervous father dotingly followed along.

As they reached the door to the maternity ward Henry grabbed his wife's arm and said,

"It's going to be okay."

Rose patted Henry's face and smiled. The nurses quickly placed Rose onto a birthing bed and attached several monitors to record her vitals and the baby's. As Rose's contractions increased in intensity she cried out several times,

"Please give me something for the pain!!"
her face contorted with discomfort.

Before long Dr. Ahmed entered the room. He examined the printout of the vitals and discussed them with the head nurse then turned to Rose and said,

"Good morning. How are you? Are you ready for a new addition to the family?"

"Yes. Can I have something for the pain?"

"Let's wait a while. If you don't deliver within the next hour or so I will order a spinal."

Delivery was taking its time, so after two hours Dr. Ahmed ordered an epidural. Soon Rose's pain subsided and she fell asleep. Henry stroked her forehead and drifted off with her.

In the early morning Dr. Ahmed visited.

"If you don't deliver within an hour we will take the baby."

"I really can't stand this anymore."

"Come on Rose; you should be a pro at this," the doctor said with a chuckle.

Rose waved her hand at him, dismissing his comment. She then looked at Henry with an endearing smile and fell back to sleep.

After a few hours Dr. Ahmed came in and examined her uterus.

"It looks like you're almost there, but one child is in breech and we will have to flip the first child to have a normal delivery. In the event we can't flip the baby, we will have to do a C section."

CHAPTER 3

———◆———

THE FLIP WAS NOT IN THE CARDS, so at 4:00 a.m. Dr. Ahmed delivered twins by Caesarian. The nurse immediately placed the first baby, a little girl, on the birthing table to be examined. "The child is ready for you, Doctor. She's not breathing. I will start compressions."

"Call another doctor to assist with delivery of the other baby while we work on this child," the doctor ordered.

Despite all the efforts the tiny new child remained unresponsive. Clearly, the baby was stillborn. Dr. Ahmed ordered the nurse,

"Clean her up and cover her body."

After a few minutes, the baby was removed from the room. As Dr. Ahmed took over delivering the second baby from the other doctor, he observed that the breathing was irregular and at one point stopped altogether. He ordered the nurse to begin chest compressions. After two minutes the normal breathing cycle was re-established, but risks remained.

Dr. Ahmed's expression was intense. He kept calling to the nurse for a read out of the vitals. As the nurses and doctor worked feverishly to save the second child, the atmosphere in the room became extremely tense. After examining the baby Dr. Ahmed suspected that there was a problem with her lungs.

"Nurse, call ICU and request a ventilator STAT!!"

After a few minutes, ICU called to confirm the ventilator was on the way. The door opened and the nurse rolled in the machine.

All the commotion in the delivery room drew Rose's attention and she asked,

"What is happening to my babies?"

The nurse ignored the question, continuing to work on the surviving child.

As Dr. Ahmed passed her, Rose grabbed his arm and implored,

"What's going on? Are the babies okay?"

"Rose, we will talk later. Right now I need to focus on the child."

She started to question what had happened to the first child, but Dr. Ahmed walked away to discuss with the nurses from ICU what to do for the baby on the examining table.

Later, he returned and spoke with Rose.

"We are doing everything we can to save her."

"What does that mean? Will they be all right?"

"Yes. She will be okay, but it will take some time."

Rose noticed with apprehension that he kept referring to one baby, but she swallowed her fears and waited. In the meantime, the first baby's body was removed from the room adjoining maternity and taken to Pathology for examination.

As they headed out the nurse called to Rose,

"Do you have a name for her, my dear?"

"Yes, it's Toni. Can I hold her now?" The nurse said nothing and slowly left the room.

Shortly after, the nurse with the second baby in the ventilator began wheeling her out to the intensive care unit.

"And does this precious little girl have a name?"

"Yes, it's Samantha."

"What happened to my first baby?"

"You must speak to the doctor," the nurse told her.

As Rose was getting cleaned up she inquired,

"When will I be able to see my girls?"

"Probably in the morning."

"How are they doing?" Rose asked with trepidation.

"They took the second baby, Samantha, to ICU. She is a tough little girl!"

Rose started to cry.

"Dr. Ahmed left orders that you could see the baby in the morning, but now he wants you to get some rest."

CHAPTER 4

——◆——

ROSE AWOKE ABOUT 7 a.m. and called the nurse. "Can I see Samantha?"

The nurse called ICU and they suggested she come down about 9 a.m. Rose breathed quick, shallow breaths ... it seemed like an eternity waiting for the time to pass.

Nine o'clock rolled around and Rose was more than eager see Samantha. As they wheeled her down the hallway and into ICU, the nurse took great pains to explain what the baby might look like –

"Now don't you go getting upset, sweetheart."

Rose entered the ICU and gasped when she saw her baby. It seemed that tubes were coming out of all her orifices. Tears started to stream down Rose's face. The nurse gently touched her shoulder and said,

"She will be okay."

Later that night Henry visited Samantha. After a few minutes, he had to leave, overcome with emotion. Rose told her husband,

"It's all right; I know our Samantha will make it."

Henry opened his mouth to speak, but could not; he nodded his head.

Rose softly told Henry,

"Our baby Samantha's sister was Toni; her precious little body was donated to research."

Henry had no comment and just stared into space.

The next day he brought their other daughters to visit their mother and they wanted to see the new baby. As they entered the room they asked,

"Can we see Samantha?"

"Not at this time, girls. It would be better for you to see her when she comes home, not in the ICU."

Then Rose sat the girls down and explained that Samantha's sister had died at birth.

"What was her name, mommy?"

"Toni."

Each day Rose would visit Samantha, with enough love in her heart for both babies. She held her in her arms and liltingly crooned old Scottish and Irish songs. Samantha seemed to respond to the softness of Rose's voice and would fall asleep.

CHAPTER 5

—◆—

D R. AHMED TOLD ROSE THE BABY WAS READY TO GO home ... finally, after two months.

Rose was overjoyed and immediately called her husband.

"Henry, guess what? Samantha can go home. Isn't that great!"

"Really! When?"

"Later this week. The hospital said Tuesday or Thursday."

"Do you think Jean would be willing to pick you up?"

"I think so, but you know how she is after the argument you had with her. Are you sure, Henry?"

"I'm sure, Rose. All I care about is getting our baby home, and it's so hard for me to get off work. So, if Jean can pick you up, that is best."

Rose called Jean and told her all about Samantha being released from the hospital.

"How is her breathing?" Jean asked.

Rose assured her sister,

"It is getting better."

Jean finally agreed to pick Rose up after some encouragement and assurances that Henry would not mind.

The next morning Rose was getting ready to leave the hospital. The weather was extremely cold and there was a 60% chance of snow. The nurse advised Rose,

"You'd better bundle her up."

Rose completed all of the forms and said goodbye to Dr. Ahmed.

"I want to see Samantha in two weeks, and don't forget to keep the vaporizer on all day in her room."

"Yes, doctor."

As Jean prepared to leave for Harris to pick up Rose and the baby, she thought about her long-standing feud with Henry resulting in her not seeing Rose for many months. It was caused by an argument with Henry yelling at Rose and Jean interceding. Jean called him an "insensitive bully" because she thought he made her sister feel so bad.

Henry then yelled at Jean,

"You're not welcome in my house!"

"That's just fine with me," Jean barked back.

But today it was different … today it was all about Samantha.

After Jean pulled her car up to the front door of the hospital she got out and started looking for Rose. Rose in turn saw Jean and brought Samantha out in a car seat. She was dressed in a pink bunting with a pink hat. The carrier was covered with so many blankets it looked empty.

Jean asked Rose,

"Where is the baby?"

"She's in here somewhere."

They both started laughing. Rose opened the door of the car, placed the carrier on the seat, adjusted the belts and took her place next to Samantha.

During the trip home from the hospital Jean and Rose laughed and giggled like the good old days before Jean and Henry's altercation.

As the car arrived home there was Henry and the four girls standing on the front stoop. Jean mumbled to herself,

"He was not supposed to be here."

The girls started yelling and waving their arms and play fighting with each other. They knew this was a big day for their new sister Samantha; she was home finally.

As Rose and Samantha got out of the car they were greeted by Henry and Samantha's sisters. Henry said "thank you" to Jean and she nodded her head. He then kissed Rose.

"I am glad you're both home."

The girls fought by shoving each other back and forth to be the first to hold the baby, insisting,

"It's my turn."

Finally Rose said,

"Each of you will have a turn, but not now. Samantha needs to rest."

Rose then gave her sister a kiss and thanked her. Jean pulled away, waving to the girls, and headed out.

As Rose took Samantha to her room she whispered to her,

"Today you will take your place as the youngest of five girls in the Jones family. But I know there are great things in your future. You will be our star."

CHAPTER 6

—◆—

IT WAS SAMANTHA'S FACIAL FEATURES that everyone noticed: her long eyelashes, her blue eyes, blondish hair and a smile that could light up the room.

Henry, a highway supervisor and a giant of a man, was taken by his daughter. Her baby noises, cooing, grunts, ahhs, and her infectious smile when Henry picked her up melted his hard shell. At night, he would sit and rock Samantha until she fell asleep. Rose would scold Henry saying, "You're spoiling her."

But Henry continued. As Samantha grew in age, her relationship with her father grew stronger. She would cater to him by making his favorite snack, or getting him a cold glass of iced tea when he came home from work. But it was the small pecks on the cheek or the stroking of his head that made all the difference. The girls would often tease her about being "Daddy's girl."

In her early days at Livingston Manor Elementary School, Samantha, nicknamed "Sam" by her classmates, achieved outstanding grades and praise from her teachers.

Henry was especially proud of his daughter's performance in math and science and had dreams of her becoming a doctor.

Samantha finished first in the New York Science Contest. Henry, who very seldom attended events, went to the medal ceremony. In fact, he arrived 30 minutes early.

As Samantha advanced to high school, her popularity followed her. She was a social butterfly and spent much of her time with friends. This often brought criticism from her sisters,

"Don't you care enough about us to do things together? We are family, you know."

When her sisters and she were at odds she would flash those "baby blues" and gently kiss them on the cheek. They could barely remember why they were mad.

In addition to her natural popularity, she needed no effort to excel academically; Samantha always achieved her goals. It was the visit by the recruiter from New York University that impressed Henry the most. Henry, Rose and Samantha met and discussed early acceptance and the possibility of entering the pre-med program.

Henry, who very seldom asked any questions, asked a number ranging from tuition and board to what was the family's responsibility. When the recruiter told them there was a possibility that Samantha could get a full scholarship, Henry beamed from ear to ear. Rose just listened and nodded in agreement. Samantha was becoming the star she had envisioned. The one caveat was that she would have to maintain her grades in math and science and her overall standing in the class.

"That should be easy," said Henry.

The next day at work, Henry told everyone about the visit from New York University and the possibility of Samantha getting a full scholarship. Henry proudly repeated the story over and over again.

Chapter 7

———◆———

At age 16, Samantha's life started changing. Her attitude became combative. She refused to listen to her mother and argued with her father all the time about school. She told Henry on multiple occasions she had no interest in becoming a doctor.

Samantha turned her attention instead to booze, boys, cars and parties. Her grades suffered and respect for her teachers declined. Several times during the school year she was threatened with suspension.

Rose and Henry became concerned about their daughter's behavior. The school suggested she see a psychologist. Despite Samantha's objection Rose set up an appointment. After completing the examination, it was determined that Samantha suffered from ADHD and was subject to bouts of depression. This was a terrible blow to Rose and Henry, but the therapist assured them it was controllable with medicine.

The tension came to a climax when she received her third quarter report card from the school. She brought it home and tried to avoid showing her father.

"Did you get a report card?"

"Yes. But … well … it's not good."

"Why?"

"Because the teachers are too hard on me."

As Henry read the report card he yelled,

"You failed math and science. How could you do that? It says 'lack of effort.' What's going on, Sam?"

She responded, "Nothing, I will try harder."

"You better or you will be grounded for the semester. Don't you realize your scholarship is on the line?"

"I do."

"Have you been taking your medication?"

"Yes," she snapped.

But Samantha was lying. The medicine made her sick so instead she spit it down the sink.

CHAPTER 8

———◆———

S AMANTHA CALLED SUSAN, her closest friend. Susan was
an average student and had little interest in school, but
together they had fun.

"What are you doing?" Samantha asked.

"Nothing special. What do you want to do?"

"How about meeting me at the diner for breakfast."

"Sure; about nine o'clock."

"Who pays?" asked Samantha.

"It's my treat."

"That's great!"

Samantha was the first to arrive at the diner and took a
seat in the booth facing the front door. She tapped her foot as
she waited for Susan to arrive and her thoughts drifted to the
upcoming party to which she was invited at Homeboys Lounge.
As Susan came through the front door Sam yelled out,

"Over here."

Susan nodded.

As Susan got closer Samantha could see she was not her
normal bouncy self.

"Where were you last night, Miss Susan?"

"I went to a party and I'm still recovering from a hang-over."

"It must have been a hard night," Sam commented as she looked at Susan's pale face.

"This is the fourth night of partying. I have to stop. Are you going to the party tonight?" Susan asked her friend.

"Yes."

Susan looked at her with intrigue,

"I have a friend home from college and he wants to meet you."

"Is he cute?" Samantha inquired, her eyes brightening.

Susan gave her the thumbs up.

As they finished breakfast they discussed their sex life and the boys involved. With the influence of 'free love' in the '60's, the two friends openly talked about sex and were caught up in the best ways to have fun. Susan, the more experienced of the two, took great pleasure in bragging about the details of her escapades. Samantha dutifully filed them away, thinking of when she would get her own experiences and 'wow' Susan.

Later that night as Samantha was getting ready to go to the party her father called her into the kitchen.

"How are you doing this quarter?"

"I am doing fine."

"What does that mean, Sam?"

"It means I am passing all my subjects," Samantha said with defiance.

"I am glad," said Henry, barely camouflaging his sarcasm.

Samantha didn't miss the barb and knew the key to charming her father was to give him a kiss on the forehead.

She smiled as she pecked him and touched his hair, then left to meet Susan.

Samantha and Susan arrived at the party at eight o'clock. The music was blaring and the house was packed with people -- downstairs, upstairs and on the lawn. Because the party was crowded it took a while before they found Peter who was dancing outside on the grass with not just one, but several girls.

Peter introduced himself as an engineering student at MIT. He had blonde hair and a great smile and was very athletic looking from playing soccer. It was an instant match between Samantha and Peter. As Susan observed the chemistry, she decided to leave them alone. She was attracted by an old friend who was waving to get her attention.

"Have a good time," said Susan to Sam and Peter.

CHAPTER 9

—◆—

"WOULD YOU LIKE A BEER?" Samantha looked up at Peter through her long eyelashes and said,

"No, but I will take a ginger ale. Thank you, Peter."

As they sat on the couch getting to know each other Samantha told Peter about her early acceptance possibilities to the NYU Medical Program.

Peter was impressed and asked,

"Wow ... early acceptance .... How old are you, Samantha?"

"Oh, I'm 18. I expect to take NYU advanced placement classes this semester, then after high school graduation this year, continue on at NYU," Samantha lied.

"Do you know in what field of medicine you want to practice?" Peter continued, satisfied that Samantha was not underage.

"No, but I am leaning towards family medicine."

Peter was captivated by her lovely features and clear intelligence and wanted to get closer.

"Would you like to dance?"

"Yes."

The two of them made their way to the place cleared for a dance floor holding each other's hands. The music was slow and it gave Peter a chance to tell Samantha about himself, his school and the career he planned after MIT. She responded with interested, intuitive comments; Peter had no clue of her young age. Sam's practicing with Susan was working.

"So, with an aerospace engineering degree, does that mean you could be an astronaut someday?"

"Maybe," said Peter.

They continued to talk and dance the night away.

"Are you ready for a beer yet?"

"Yes. I'll have a Coors."

Samantha heaved a little sigh of relief as Peter went to get the drink, glad she remembered what she thought was a cool-sounding beer.

Peter kept bringing Samantha Coors and beer for himself and the hours wore on as they were drinking and dancing. Before long, both were unable to function normally. They were tiring from partying.

They found a couch to sit and relax, discuss how much fun the party was and that they were looking forward to the next one. Peter placed his arm around Samantha's shoulder and pulled her toward him. She hesitated at first, but eventually let Peter kiss her.

The first kiss was short and not very impressive. The second kiss was long and passionate and aroused Samantha's new sexual feelings. She loved the sensation and wanted more. She responded by kissing Peter, several times on the lips, almost as if she were pecking him, then kissing his ears and neck and placing her tongue in his ear. Samantha then proceeded to kiss him passionately on the mouth for several minutes.

The conversations about sex that Samantha had with Susan did not include what she was learning now, that feeling free enough to arouse her partner would arouse her as well. Samantha's passion heightened with the long foreplay and the mystery of giving pleasure. This clearly excited both of them and Peter began pulling Samantha's hair back and kissing her on the neck.

He suggested they go upstairs to the bedroom, but Samantha said,

"No, I just met you."

Peter replied, "It seems I have known you for years."

The age-old come-on was new to Samantha, so after an hour or so of passionate exchanges and some coaxing, she agreed to go to the bedroom and watched Peter's tight behind as he lead her up the stairs.

As Samantha and Peter laid on the bed, Peter pulled her closer to him pressing his warm body against hers. He rubbed her back and unhooked her bra. As they exchanged soft and intense kisses Peter tried to unbutton her jeans. Samantha could feel the heat from Peter's hand tracing her ears and the curve of her chin, running his finger along her shoulders, rubbing her breasts and slowly making his way to her stomach. He stroked her inner thighs and she finished unbuttoning her jeans to invite him. He prolonged her desire by slowly pulling her jeans down to her knees.

Samantha feigned resistance with a weak, unbelievable, "Stop," which Peter ignored.

Samantha was so excited that the warmth of Peter's body caused her to lose all perspective. After Peter removed her jeans, he slowly rolled down the top of her panties. With each roll, he kissed her breasts then slowly licked his way to her navel. The wet, passionate kisses and Peter's gentle sucking of her lower lip caused Samantha to thrust and heave her body in the age-old rhythmic dance of excitement with which we are born. She could hardly stand the anticipation of what was to come.

Finally, Peter removed her panties and got on top of her. Samantha slowly raised her hips from the bed to meet Peter's engorged penis. He grabbed each side of her buttocks and spread her legs apart as he slowly pushed into her body.

"Oh, my God; so, this is how it feels ... wet and wild and taken," Samantha thought to herself.

She was so moist with passion, but little things caused Peter to wonder if she was a virgin. As he thrust himself in and then out repeatedly both Peter and Samantha groaned with enjoyment. Peter could not hold back any longer and finally climaxed in Samantha; she loved the closeness and knowing that she excited him so much, but she did not experience an orgasm this first time, only making her want more soon.

Gradually, Peter rolled off of Samantha and onto the bed. She lay motionless saying nothing. They both tried to catch their breaths, then resumed kissing as they lay side by side.

Peter asked, "are you ok?"

CHAPTER 10

———◆———

T HE QUESTION BROUGHT SAMANTHA OUT of the dream
and back into reality and she immediately pulled the
covers over her naked body. She paused for a moment, looked
up at him as though questioning and said, "Yes."

Peter asked her,

"Was this your first time?"

Samantha turned slightly away and said with a touch of
embarrassment,

"Yes."

The gifted and talented beautiful young teenager was no
longer a virgin ... she was a party girl in the 60's. She laid on
the bed silently looking at the ceiling, thinking about the consequences of her actions.

"What a mistake I made," she thought, slipping into
visions of the traditional values she had been taught.

"How cheap I must appear after meeting him for the
first time. What if I got pregnant?"

The more she thought about what happened the worse
she felt.

"Do you want me to take you home?"

Samantha said "No," imagining a sign over his head announcing to her parents that he had taken her. They could be up when she was not yet home and dawn was peeping through the darkness. She found her way to the party without Peter and she could find her way home without Peter.

"Samantha, the first time can be a wonderful memory, and things will be even better in the future. I will call you next week," Peter promised.

"Okay."

Peter indeed called later that week telling her that he was planning to come home from Boston and he wanted to take her out. Samantha told him that she had to study for a test. Peter tried to convince her to go, but she was steadfast, thinking that some resistance might balance out him thinking she was 'easy.'

CHAPTER 11

———◆———

S AMANTHA EXPERIENCED SICKNESS and severe weight gain during the next few weeks. Peter would call ever so often, but with the passing of time and the changes in her body, she showed very little interest.

Samantha attributed the weight gain to the medication she was taking, but in reality she did not have a period in two months.

Rose would joke about how Samantha was the healthiest of all the girls and the medicine was the cause of her gaining weight; however, her sisters suspected otherwise. Despite Samantha's denial of any irregularity, her complaints of morning sickness with the occasional vomiting provided her sisters with the facts they needed.

As the weight gain and morning sickness were of particular concern to Rose she asked Samantha several times if she had gotten her period. On each occasion, she lied, "yes." But Samantha was conerned that time was running out and her parents would learn if she were pregnant. She prayed this was just a medical aberration.

Rose's concern was growing and without Samantha's knowledge, she scheduled an examination with Doctor Ahmed. On the day before Rose told her daughter about the appointment.

Samantha was furious, "Mother, I am not going to see a doctor."

"Then I will have to tell your father and you can explain it to him."

Despite continuing objections, Samantha gave in to her mother and went to the appointment. They entered the doctor's office and were escorted to the examination room. Samantha put on a dressing gown and sat on the edge of the table.

After examining Samantha, Dr. Ahmed asked about her sexual activity. Samantha stole a look at Rose and croaked out, "None."

Dr. Ahmed then asked her about the morning sickness.

"This is overblown, Doctor. I threw up only once in the morning."

Rose interrupted and said,

"That's wrong, Samantha. You know it's happened on a number of days."

Samantha was silent and looked down at the floor.

Dr. Ahmed asked her again the same question regarding her sexual activity.

"I have had no sexual activity. Don't you believe me!"

Rose was silent. Dr. Ahmed continued the examination of her neck, ears, throat and breasts that were slightly swollen and sensitive.

The doctor then suggested that they run a series of tests.

"Would you mind taking a pregnancy test?"

Samantha knew it would be worse to refuse, so she said, "Yes. But why do you want me to?"

"Just so I can rule out all possible causes."

"I told you I did not have sexual intercourse,"

But because of the symptoms, Rose pushed for the test. A little voice inside of Samantha said, "That's it, Sam," and she gave in to her mother. Samantha's ability to hide her condition was coming to a close and she was not sure what to do or who to tell.

A week later the doctor's office called to speak with Rose while she was out. When Samantha heard the message on the old answering machine, she called the doctor's office back asking for the lab department. Samantha, posing as Rose, listened to the nurse who gave her the results. After confirming the pregnancy there was complete silence … no conversation at all.

"Are you there?"

A gulp and a "Yes" was the only word spoken, terminating the call.

As she hung up the phone, she looked at her mother who just walked into the room and asked,

"Who was on the phone?"

"The doctor's office."

"What were the results? Was it the medicine that added water weight?"

Samantha shook her head and in a low voice said, "no, Mom."

"What was it, Samantha?" said Rose, appearing agitated by the delay in answering her question.

Samantha lowered her head and left the room without any explanation.

CHAPTER 12

—◆—

"WHAT'S WRONG? ARE YOU SICK?" said Rose, following her daughter.

After a few minutes of silence and not answering the question, Samantha said with distress,

"Oh, Mom. I'm pregnant."

Rose's face turned pale and the sweat beads on her forehead showed her concern.

"Maybe it's a mistake."

"No, it's not!"

"What do you mean?" said Rose with a mother's disbelief even though she had known the symptoms clearly pointed to this.

"I had sex with Peter. I just wanted to be like the other kids at the party. Everybody has sex these days. He was so nice, and he's an engineering student at MIT even. Oh, Mom."

"When?"

"At the party two months ago."

"You don't even know this boy."

"I made a mistake."

"How am I going to tell your father?" Rose said in a dejected voice, as she sat down on the chair and slumped into the cushion.

"How did it happen?"

Samantha did not answer. Rose started crying.

Samantha went up to her room and called Susan. As the phone rang Samantha tried to figure out what to say.

"Hi" said Susan. "What's up?"

"I'm in trouble."

"What kind?"

A pause, then, "I'm going to have a baby."

Samantha could hear her swallow, then Susan said,

"Holy shit. Are you sure?"

Samantha squeaked out, "Yes, the doctor's office just confirmed the lab results."

"Have you told your parents?"

"My mother knows, but not my father."

"Have you told Peter?"

Samantha screeched out, then lowered her voice,

"No! I have to go. I'll call you later, Susan."

"Make sure you do."

Samantha hung up the phone.

Later Peter called,

"I am home for the weekend; where do you want to go to dinner? How about Richie's?"

"That sounds great. What time?"

"About 7:30," Peter said, happy she agreed to see him again after so long and remembering tracing her every curve.

Samantha was the first to arrive and Peter followed a few minutes later. He kissed her on the cheek but sensed something was wrong.

"Hey Peter; what's up. How is school?"

"It's good; how about you?"

Samantha avoided the question, then after taking a deep breath she said,

"I have a surprise for you."

Peter grinned, "Is it a present?"

"No."

"What then?"

"You are going to be a father, Peter," Samantha announced with some reservation."

Peter's grin disappeared as though a page in a book turned.

"It can't be!"

Neither of them spoke as the minutes ticked by. Peter was the first to break the heavy silence.

"You are going to ruin my life, Samantha."

"What about my life?" she retorted thinking how predictably self-centered Peter was.

He tried to explain,

"You haven't started college yet. I told you all about my plans. How am I going to handle getting an engineering degree at MIT and a family? What are we going to do? How do I even know it's mine?"

"I told you I was a virgin, Peter. I have never slept with anyone else."

"How do I know that for sure?"

Samantha threw her glass of water into Peter's face,

"Because I said so. You are a fucking asshole."

"I have an answer," said Peter wiping the water from his face.

"Get an abortion."

"No. Are you kidding."

"Don't worry; I will pay for it."

"I don't care who pays for it; I am not going to kill my child."

"Well, speaking of 'killing'; my parents are going to kill me. What about my career? I have just been accepted into the Space Program. I can't take on this responsibility. I have two more years of school before I graduate. Do you want money? Tell me what you want me to do?"

"Screw you. I will take care of myself and my baby. Don't call me ever again."

She then proudly walked out of the restaurant, her head held high, tossing her lovely blond hair that curled down her back.

CHAPTER 13

⬥

S AMANTHA WAS SHOWING despite her stories of 'putting on weight due to the medicine.' It was obvious she was pregnant and would have to tell her father.

That night at the dinner table, her father said,

"Samantha, are you gaining more weight?"

"Yes, Dad. I have not been watching my diet."

"Did you go to the doctor last month?"

"Yes."

"What did he say?"

Samantha was silent. Rose tried to buy a little time,

"We have not heard from the doctor yet. We should get the results soon."

"Why so long?" Henry inquired with puzzlement.

"They have to send one test out to Albany," Rose added a little too quickly.

"Do you think you are pregnant?" then he laughed at his own joke.

Everyone else at the table looked away.

Samantha paused then said, "Dad, we need to talk."

"Then let's talk now."

"Dad, what I have to say will be very upsetting."

"What do you mean?"

"Well, I have a medical condition … it's hard to tell you."

"What medical condition? Are you ill? Does your mother know about it?"

Rose looked down towards the floor.

"Somebody tell me what is going on, and I mean right now before I get pissed off!"

Samantha announced in a loud voice,

"You weren't joking, Dad. That's why nobody laughed. I'm pregnant!"

Henry sat back in his chair then spoke to Rose,

"You knew about this?"

Rose was silent; she was her star's mother.

Henry stood up, threw his napkin on his dinner plate and walked into the living room. Samantha was stunned, but understood her father's reaction. Rose asked the girls to go up to their rooms.

Henry's disappointment approaching anger was written all over his face. His dreams for Samantha were over … no scholarship to NYU … no medical school. As he sat back into his chair he could feel the pressure in his chest. He called out to Rose,

"Get me an aspirin please."

Later on, Samantha's father called her into the living room. She started apologizing, but her father put up his hand and stopped her.

"How could you do this? What were you thinking? You might be only 16, but if you knew enough to do this you should know enough to use protection, Samantha."

Samantha explained she was drunk and a virgin.

"Oh, great … drunk …. The boy, what does he say?"

Henry, like many in the county, did not pursue trying for a shotgun wedding, or even bringing up the subject of child support which would take time from Henry's job to go to court to petition and possibly hiring an attorney, which he could not afford. No, he preferred to keep Social Services out of it. With Samantha's young age, even the Child Protection Agency could get involved and start an investigation into why Samantha was out all night, drinking and sleeping around … where were her parents. No, he would do nothing that might cause snooping around.

Samantha answered with a chip on her shoulder,

"He wants me to get an abortion. I said, No!"

"Why not?" Henry asked, grasping for straws to save the dreams he had for his smart, beautiful baby girl.

"I am not going to kill my child. Is that how you raised me?" Samantha challenged.

"There are some practicalities here, young lady. How are you going to take care of the child?"

"I will get a job and mom can watch the baby. Maybe I can go to school at night and finish high school," Samantha said, knowing that any other pregnant girls she had heard of dropped out of school; a sense of shame still prevailed.

Henry's eyes were welling up and tears started running down his face. There was the family to consider. And there were risks, however unlikely.

CHAPTER 14

❖

"I KNOW THIS SOUNDS CRUEL, Samantha, but I must set an example for your sisters. I want you to leave our house."

Samantha sat back in the chair stunned by her father's words.

"Where do I go? What do I do?"

Her father was silent, then stuck in a barb.

"If you are old enough to get pregnant then you are old enough to live on your own."

Everyone in the house was shocked. Rose started crying. As Samantha dejectedly went to her bedroom with the emptiness of the loss of her father's support, Rose said to her,

"Honey, I will talk to him. Let me deal with your father."

Later that night after everyone was thought to be asleep, Samantha could hear the sound of her parents arguing.

"She disappointed me. How could she do this? She had a bright future and she threw it away for a drunken one-night stand. Why didn't you say something to me?"

Rose was silent.

As Samantha listened through the vents in her bed-room, the tears rolled down her cheeks. Then she heard her father say,

"I will give her to the end of next month to find a place to live."

Rose objected strenuously, but Henry insisted.

"She betrayed me. She must go. What kind of an example would I set for the other girls if I let her stay here?"

Rose was inclined to be a traditional wife and follow her husband's wishes; however, she imagined the pain their daughter Samantha, her star, could experience in their home knowing she had been kicked out, just waiting for the last day. Rose took immediate action and called her sister Jean, Henry's nemesis.

CHAPTER 15

—⇒◆⇐—

R OSE TOOK SAMANTHA ASIDE the next morning and told her that her father would not change his mind. Samantha started to cry. Rose wiped away the tears from Samantha's cheeks and tried to comfort her daughter with,

"I discussed the pregnancy with your Aunt Jean last night, and she is willing to let you stay with her until the baby is born, or maybe longer if necessary."

Jean lived on Chestnut Street in Liberty, 20 minutes from Livingston Manor. She and Henry did not like each other. So, Jean felt that doing this favor for Rose and his pride and joy Samantha would result in getting back at Henry. She loved every minute of imagining making him squirm knowing she was helping Samantha when he had refused.

The old saying, 'the leaf doesn't fall far from the tree' was true for Sam … she was like her mother and eager to leave rather than live in her home. To stay, even until her father's deadline, would be a blow to her self-respect because she had gone from being the daughter of whom he was so proud to the daughter of whom he was so ashamed. Living with her Aunt

Jean would be the first step towards becoming independent. She would show her father … she would show them all … she would become someone her father would love again.

The day Samantha left the home was painful for the whole family. As she and her sisters packed her clothes you could hear their crying and expressions of anger.

"Why do you have to leave?"

Again and again the question was asked …

"Why? Why? Why?"

Samantha kissed her sisters goodbye as they tried to hold back their tears. She then kissed her father and he wiped his wet cheeks and tried to keep a stern face.

"I will always be a Daddy's girl. I love you."

Henry was silent.

"I will let you know when the baby is born," Sam said, still trying to get her father to speak.

But he could not … the lump in his throat was too big … the needs to be a stern parent and to show tough love were a brick wall. Henry had no response as the tears streamed from his eyes.

"Be safe, my darling," he whispered to himself.

CHAPTER 16

——✦——

R OSE WAS SOBBING as she told Samantha, "I'll take you to your Aunt Jean's house in Liberty now."

While driving the truck she discussed what she planned to do to help her daughter salvage her life in some way.

"I will send you money each month."

"Can I bring the baby to see you?" asked Samantha.

"Let's wait until it's born," said her mother.

Jean met Rose and Samantha at the door and took them into the house offering them tea. After a while Rose kissed Samantha and told her she loved her. Jean and Rose walked to the car and spoke privately.

"Take care of Samantha for me, Jeannie," said Rose.

"I will," she said to her sister with fervent commitment.

As the due date got closer for the birth of Samantha's baby, Rose and her sisters started planning a shower in Liberty at the firehouse to try and bring some joy into the predicament. They invited a number of family and friends, including Samantha's girlfriends.

Just before the date of the baby shower Rose and Henry

had a terrible argument over Samantha coming back to live at their family home after the baby was born. Henry refused to allow any discussion of the subject. But what stunned them all was his adamant demand,

"Rose, you and the girls are forbidden to go to that baby shower. This is certainly not an occasion to celebrate!"

Rose mounted a fierce defense, even threatening to leave, but Henry would not hear of any arguments. He felt that in his position as head of the family, it was his decision and it was final. Rose saw it as a blow to Samantha's self-worth and any chance for her to have the confidence to make a life for herself.

"How can you possibly feel this way after what you experienced before we were married?"

"Rose, I don't want to talk about it; that was a long time ago."

INTERLUDE

—◆—

"A LONG TIME AGO," THE MAN'S WIFE SAID, then replied,

"An attorney just called and wants to meet with us."

"What does he want?"

"He didn't say."

"I hope he's not looking for money."

"I doubt it," she said, a sound of disgust in her voice.

After a long pause, "okay."

She called the attorney back and they confirmed the time and place.

At 7:00 p.m. he pulled his dark grey, almost black, BMW into the front yard. The woman was already standing on the porch stairs. As he got out of his car, he greeted her then followed her into the house.

As he entered, an air of familiarity overcame him … like he'd been there before. A large, robust man was sitting in his recliner and nodded as the attorney came through the door and took a seat on the couch.

"I am very sorry for your loss."

Neither the man or the woman responded.

"As you know, the court approved the adoption."

"Why are you telling us?"

"I would like to propose a plan in order to get the children returned to you."

The woman looked at her husband, but both were silent.

The attorney asked, "Are you interested in getting custody?"

The woman looked at the man's face and it was expressionless. She said nervously, "Of course."

The man raised his hand as if to stop his wife from speaking, then said, "We can't."

"These are your granddaughters."

"We just can't."

The woman stared at the floor and was silent.

The man said to the attorney,

"We'd love to, but it's not possible."

The attorney's face reflected his frustration and he was sure they had no interest in the children. After their decision, he exchanged small talk with them and answered the perfunctory questions about his background.

"I grew up on the west coast but was born in Livingston Manor. I was adopted."

The woman asked, "Did you know your birth mother?"

The attorney surprised the man and the woman with, "Yes. But she passed away."

"Sorry to hear that. What was her name may I ask?"

The attorney gave her name absentmindly and added,

"She lived on Candlestick Road."

The man was silent and studied the attorney's face with great intensity. The woman also starred at him. He concluded his conversation and left.

The man and the woman stared at each other. Then the woman said,

"He is your son."

The man could hardly speak. The attorney was his daughter's brother; the child he had given up for adoption. Deja vu.

"I can't believe it."

He got up from his chair and went upstairs to his room.

CHAPTER 17

———◆———

"AUNT JEAN, MY WATER BROKE," Samantha called out on the sixth day of September.

"Get your bags and let's go."

As Samantha sat in the front seat, all the challenges she had experienced flashed through her mind. What kind of a life would her child have? All along, the labor pains increased in intensity and the intervals shortened.

As they arrived at Harris Hospital, Jean parked in the ambulance space, got out and started yelling for help. Two nurses came running from inside the emergency room.

"My niece's water broke; she's having a baby. The labor pains are getting close together!"

They helped Samantha into a wheel chair and rapidly took her off to maternity.

The next morning Samantha surprised everyone, including herself, by delivering not one, but two girls. Jean was excited as she watched the twins being born. She called Rose,

"Well, sis, you're a grandmother."

"That's great! But why didn't you call me sooner?"

"It was all I could do to get Samantha to the hospital in time. But there's a bigger surprise ... you have twin grandchildren!"

"Are you kidding?" Rose expressed with disbelief.

"No, for real. And they are both beautiful, with blonde hair, and it looks like they will have blue eyes, just like Samantha. I will call you later. By the way, when are you going to visit Samantha?"

"I can't, Jean; it's a problem for Henry."

"What an ass," was all Jean could say as she hung up the phone.

Despite the joy of the twins being born, there was no joy at the Jones household. Time passed. The family had an empty place at the table where the precocious Samantha had always sat. No one spoke of her when Henry was present.

When the twins were ten months old and learning to walk, Samantha discussed the idea of moving out. Jean was disappointed because she loved the twins and she treated them as if they were her own. But as she had gotten to know Samantha and taken to her, she understood.

"Where do you plan to go?" asked Jean.

"I'm not sure."

Jean suggested that Samantha contact the Salvation Army.

Samantha called them, "Do you have any open apartments?"

"Yes, one just opened up."

"I will be right there,"

She was in luck; they had an open apartment in town.

"Now, I can start a life of my own with my children."

CHAPTER 18

———◆———

SAMANTHA MOVED HER TWINS Jodi and Angel into a run-down apartment house at 122 Academy Street. The apartment windows overlooked an abandoned lot filled with grass, weeds, pieces of used machinery, beer bottles, tires and assorted junk. But to Samantha, a 17-year-old unwed mother with new hope for the future, it was a view from the top. She was independent; she could do what she believed in.

The apartment had two bedrooms, a living room, bath and a kitchen. The bath had holes in the wall exposing pipes and the tile was peeling off the plywood floor. But to Samantha, this was home, and she would make something special of it.

'Special' took on a new definition. It was special to be a mother of two little girls under a year old with no one to help. Special to have no occupational skills or training. Special to have no family support to care for the children so she could continue her education or get any type of a job. Special to try to get up every morning and keep going when she felt so down and had no depression meds. Samantha felt special … specially bad. Then she looked into the mirror and announced to herself,

"I have to get some money no matter what it takes."

CHAPTER 19

THERE WAS AN UNKEMPT, YOUNG MAN slumping, wearing a psychedelic shirt and a bandana on his head. While the girls were sleeping Samantha slipped out to the corner where she noticed him and decided he wasn't bad looking. He smiled at her and she answered when he spoke to her.

"What is your name?" she asked, smiling back.

"Bobby Mcgee," he answered with a grin showing slightly discolored teeth ... one missing.

"Sure; and I'm Janis Joplin."

He offered a swig of his warm beer wrapped in a brown paper bag. He seemed harmless, so she invited him to her nearby apartment ... she had to get back right away in case her little girls woke up.

Bobby's real name was Hua. He got down on the floor and played with Sam's daughters and said her apartment could be very nice if she had a little help. The beat was on. She invited Hua to move in.

During drinking episodes that were all too frequent, Hua told of his past, his oriental parents, his failed dreams of becoming famous for martial arts and blending in boxing and wrestling. When he drank, he practiced beating Samantha. Although each time he pleaded for forgiveness from the lovely blond sexy woman, it would always happen again. Sam threw him out. And with Hua went his help with the expenses.

Samantha went through other debilitating house-sharing experiences then called Susan to brainstorm.

"Well, with your looks and my moxie, maybe we could act like hookers and get away with the money before anything happened."

That ended up as a debacle which could have been predicted, and they were lucky the undercover police officer they approached let them off with a stern warning.

Samantha's creativity and determination the first Friday after that resulted in another episode with the police asking her questions about pushing Mary Jane. It was time to try something less risky.

CHAPTER 20

—⋙◆⋘—

SAMANTHA PLASTERED FLYERS throughout the Town and Village of Liberty, announcing a house party for just five dollars per person, BYOB. The townspeople were always happy to have something to do that did not cost much. They were also curious to go to the home of the striking, personable young blond with the adorable twins.

The attendance was overwhelming. There were so many people that some could not get into the apartment so they chose to stand in the hallway or hang out on the porch. But wherever they were, Samantha considered them party guests. Motorcyclists raced their bikes up and down Academy until the wee hours of the morning. The music was so loud that the party goers could hear it in the street, and dancing was wherever they could find a spot to move their feet.

Samantha could be seen in her boots, jeans and wide-brimmed straw cowboy hat with a beaver tail, collecting admissions. One party goer said,

"No, I'm not paying any $5.00; I'm just standing here on

the stoop," but Samantha convinced him that counted and he coughed up the five spot.

Despite all the blaring music, the first visit from police was not until one-thirty in the morning. The patrolman slowly made his way up the stairwell and into the apartment. He asked the party goers,

"Whose apartment is this?"

They pointed to Samantha. She gaily waved to him and pushed through the crowd to talk. The patrolman saw how friendly she was and decided everyone was just having a good time. He motioned to Samantha to lower the music. She responded with a thumbs up. The officer left.

At two-thirty, after complaints about the motorcycles and loud music, three patrolmen made their way up the stairwell and into the apartment. By then, the floor was littered with leftovers and bottles; people were dozing in the corners, some were ganged up sleeping on the floor of the twins' bedroom. Samantha was lying on the couch half asleep herself.

These patrolmen were not taken with her at all.

"Okay, people. Time to leave. Come on; the party's over!"

The police cleared the partygoers out of apartment and told Samantha,

"We're leaving now, young lady."

"Okay," said Samantha.

Her reputation as a party girl was introduced and firmly established with the police and neighbors in just one night.

CHAPTER 21

—◆—

T HE STATE CENTRAL REGISTRY was called during the
week saying Samantha was neglecting her children. The
complaint was deemed "credible" and referred to Social Services in Sullivan County.

The case was assigned to Anna Frank, MSW, an experienced Social Services Investigator. Because Anna had heard
stories on the street about Samantha, she made an unan-
nounced visit to her home.

As Anna approached the apartment house she noticed
that the railings were missing. There were old flower pots
lined up on the sill of the porch which had a stained couch,
throw pillows and an end table. There were four garbage cans
outside with an apartment number painted on each can. The
trash was overflowing from the cans onto the ground.

Anna confirmed the apartment number by looking at
the mailboxes on the side of the house. She opened the front
door and was immediately taken aback by the smell inside the
hallway. The condition of the building with its falling paint
chips and holes in the wall attested to the poor condition. As

she climbed the stairs, Anna had to step over trash lying on the steps and landing.

"How could people live like this?" said Anna to herself.

As she reached the apartment, she listened for any sign of activity. Anna knocked first lightly, then with force. A person with long blond hair, shorts and a tank top partly opened the door.

"What do you want?" the girl asked.

Anna started to explain, then stopped and flashed her badge.

"So, what do you want?" the girl said again.

"I want to come in and speak with you," Anna said matter of factly.

The young woman behind the door hesitated and then opened it slowly saying,

"Come in."

As Anna entered the apartment, she was overcome by the smell of urine and cat feces overflowing from the cat box. She addressed the young woman,

"You are?"

"Samantha; just call me Sam."

"I am from Social Services, Sam. Our office received a complaint."

"Who made the complaint?"

"That's confidential."

"I bet it's the neighbor across the hall. That bitch said she would get back at me for the party."

Samantha shook her head to emphasize her disgust.

"We are following up to ensure there are no concerns about possible child abuse or neglect. Would you mind showing me the apartment?"

"Sure."

"Are there any children here?"

"Yes. They are sleeping in the bedroom."

As Sam and Anna walked from one room to another, the smell seemed to intensify. Anna made mental notes of the dishes piled high in the sink, bowls with mildew and a browning half-eaten apple lying on the center table. In Sam's bedroom was a mattress, but no sheets or blankets.

"Where do you sleep?" asked Anna.

"With the kids," Samantha said as though it should be obvious.

The floor was covered with clothes and newspapers.

"There are no shades on the window. Can't the neighbor see directly into your bedroom? Not much privacy."

"He gets a thrill once in a while. Who cares."

As Anna moved towards the next room, she could see two little girls in diapers, sleeping on a mattress. Surrounding the mattress was a small wall of clean, unfolded diapers. By the door was a pail of dirty diapers reeking with odor. In the corner of the room there were several empty bottles of Miller Light. Anna mumbled to herself,

"It looks like a training ground for cockroaches."

Just then five roaches came running across the room … Anna had seen enough.

She started walking towards the front door, as if to leave. Samantha said sarcastically,

"You're leaving so soon."

Anna turned and looked at Sam and in a stern voice admonished,

"These conditions are deplorable and a health hazard to the children."

"Bull shit; I have been sick. What do you want from me?"

"A reasonable effort on your part."

"I try."

Anna, frustrated by the whole conversation announced,

"I am going to remove the children until the conditions are resolved."

"My ass!"

Anna proceeded to the landing outside the apartment, paused and called the police.

Meanwhile, Samantha yelled at Anna,

"You are not taking my kids, you bitch. You have your own kids; don't steal mine."

While Samantha was carrying on Anna was on the phone talking to the Liberty police dispatcher telling him she was with Social Services.

"We are removing two children from the house, and I need assistance."

Within minutes Anna could hear the sirens wailing, then a patrolman entered the downstairs door and came running up the stairs. As he entered the apartment, the smell stopped him in his tracks.

"Wow!" and he staggered backwards.

The officer introduced himself,

"Hi. I am Officer Mullen."

"Watch the mother while I get the children dressed. I am planning to remove them due to the poor health conditions."

Sam, hearing the conversation, started screaming,

"Over my dead body."

Officer Mullen tried to calm her down, but there were no words possible that could have done so. Suddenly, without warning, Sam lunged at Anna to punch her in the face.

Officer Mullen quickly handcuffed Sam and marched her to the patrol car. She kept screaming and struggled to get to her twins,

"Give me back my kids!"

Anna threw clothes in a duffle bag, dressed the children and proceeded to the car. After Anna drove off, Officer Mullen opened the back door of the patrol car and told Sam to get out. He placed his hand on her head to avoid her bumping it on the car frame, then removed the handcuffs.

Sam slammed the door saying,

"Thanks for nothing."

Officer Mullen shook his head.

"She could have charged you with assault, Miss."

"Well, I am going to have her charged with kidnapping," retorted Samantha with vehemence.

The officer laughed.

As Officer Mullen drove away, Samantha went back into the apartment. Just inside, she grabbed an empty vase, encrusted with residue, and hurled it at the wall, yelling,

"Fuck you."

Anna pulled up to a white one-story home and Wanda, a foster mother, came out the front door to meet the car. The children were half asleep as Anna and Wanda picked them up, covered them with blankets and carried them into the house.

CHAPTER 22

———◆———

A WEEK AFTER THE CHILDREN were removed, Samantha
received a letter from Family Court located in Monticello,
New York, requiring her appearance to answer neglect charges
before Judge Colleen Henderson at 9:30 a.m. Samantha mumbled,
"What neglect? Dumb Asses! So I didn't clean the house.
I was sick."

Samantha called Susan.

"I just got a letter from Family Court; what should I do?"

"Sam, you have to go and find out what is happening."

"But I didn't do anything."

"It doesn't matter. The Court says come, you must show up,
period -- if not for you, then for your babies. Sam, you've always
been my best friend and I know how you love Jodi and Angel;
me too. There are things you're going to do with the Court all
the way in Monticello and I don't know who can take you every
time. My parents are giving me their car cause they're buying
another one. So I'm giving you my old truck. It might not start
easily or run all the time, but you got nothin now."

"Oh Susan. Thank you. What would I do without you."

CHAPTER 23

—◆—

S AMANTHA PUT ON A PAIR OF JEANS, a tank top and floppy sandals, got into her truck and drove to the Monticello Family Court the next morning. As she parked her truck in the Department of Motor Vehicles lot, Sam could hardly hold back her anger.

"Who do they think they are taking my kids?"

As she walked towards the one-story grey cinderblock building with a sign saying "Sullivan County Annex," she stopped to decide which door, mumbling,

"Is this a jail or a courthouse?"

Samantha chose the double doors nearest her to enter and saw the probation department on the left, a lunch room directly ahead and a long hallway with chairs lined up against the window sill on her right.

She approached a young woman sitting on a chair waiting for the probation officer.

"Where is Family Court?"

The young girl pointed to the double doors at the end of the hallway.

As Samantha opened the double doors, she was greeted by a court officer who asked,

"What is the name of the case?"

"I have an appointment with Judge Colleen Henderson."

"The name of the case please."

"I am Samantha Jones."

The court officer checked his log indicating she was scheduled before Judge Henderson.

"Take a seat. I will call you."

Shortly after, the speaker blared out: "Jones, Samantha -- Courtroom One." As Samantha got up from her seat, a feeling of anxiety suddenly washed over her. Her hands became sweaty and she felt sick to her stomach.

After a minute or two she headed for the courtroom then entered. The court officer instructed her:

"Empty the contents of your pockets into the white plastic basket, then walk under the arch of the metal detector."

As she walked under, the buzzer did not go off and she proceeded. The court officer opened the door, she entered and he escorted her to a table in front of the judge's bench.

Samantha could feel her heart beating and asked the court officer for a tissue to wipe the perspiration from her brow. Across the room she saw Anna Frank in a blue tailored suit sitting next to a bald man with a rumpled gray suit. Samantha said to herself,

"You would think he could afford a new suit."

In the back of the courtroom was a matronly woman in a print dress, eyeglasses on the bridge of her nose and a sour look on her face. Also sitting in the back row of the courtroom was an extremely well-dressed, handsome, dark-complexioned, curly-haired man.

"Well," she thought to herself with a bit of admiration and curiosity. "I wonder who he is."

Suddenly and without notice two middle-aged women entered the courtroom from the side door behind the judge's bench and took their seats.

The court officer then called the court to order:

"All Rise. This Court is now in session; The Honorable Justice Colleen Henderson presiding."

Samantha was impressed with the formality, but her heart was on overload.

CHAPTER 24

———◆———

THE JUDGE ENTERED THE COURT dressed in a black robe, her hair in a bun, a few curly strands straggling loose. Samantha thought to herself,

"What a fashion statement."

The judge asked for a roll call of participants:

Anna Frank--Social Services,

Ira Tietz--Attorney, Social Services,

Samantha Jones,

Roberta Black--Attorney for the children,

Jose Rameriz.

The judge addressed Social Services:

"I have read your petition for custodial care for the minors Jodi and Angel Jones. Do you have anything else you wish to add?"

"No, Your Honor."

The judge turned to Samantha,

"Miss Jones, do you understand why you are in court?"

"I guess."

"Well what is it, you do or you don't?"

"They took my children," Samantha's voice was cracking with emotion.

"Why, Miss Jones? Do you have any idea?"

"Because the house wasn't clean."

The judge's face said it all.

"No, Miss Jones. It's because the conditions in the house were deplorable and a threat to the children's health and welfare. Do you understand it now?"

"Yes," said Samantha in a respectful tone, now seriously worried and afraid.

"Do you have anything else to say?"

"Yes. I am a good mother and have taken good care of my babies since they were born. I admit I suffer from depression and at times it keeps me from perfectly cleaning up the apartment, or doing much of anything. But, for sure, the children have never seen me drunk. I do drink excessively at times, I know, but I plan to go to AA for help. That's good, isn't it?" she pleaded.

Samantha paused long enough for the judge to ask,

"Anything else?" with no change in her dour expression.

"Yes," said Samantha, unwilling to stop until she could get out her pleas.

"I don't have any medicine except for a few pills that I received from the emergency room several months ago. I take a pill ever so often when the depression gets bad, and then I get better. But I never get down enough to not take care of my babies. I truly love them. I swear, I am a good mother."

"Miss Jones, do you have health coverage?"

"No."

"I would advise you to see Social Services for help."

"I did Judge, but I could not figure out the papers."

"Did you ask anyone for help with the forms?"

"No," Sam blurted.

"Miss Jones, do you understand the gravity of the charges you are facing?"

"Yes," she whimpered.

"Do you understand that if convicted you could lose your parental rights?"

"For not cleaning the house?" Samantha said with disbelief and amazement!

"We are charging you with neglect."

"Who did I neglect? Not my kids!"

"Do you have a lawyer, Miss Jones?"

"No."

"Can you afford a lawyer?"

"No."

"Then a lawyer will be provided by the state."

Samantha interrupted the Judge,

"What about my kids?"

The judge ignored her question.

The ruling was to keep the children in custodial care with *no visitation for the mother.*

Samantha started crying,

"Why can't I see my baby girls?"

The Judge ignored her reaction.

"I don't understand," Sam said, now with a pathetic tone.

"You need a lawyer, Miss Jones. Let's set the pre-trial hearing for two weeks."

Social Services agreed.

As Samantha left the courtroom, the judge yelled out,

"Miss Jones, the next time you appear in my court, dress appropriately."

As Samantha was leaving, she walked behind Anna Frank from Social Services. She whispered to Anna,

"Someday, you will get yours."

CHAPTER 25

———◆———

S AMANTHA LEFT THE COURTROOM and called Susan to
tell her about the hearing in Family Court.

"Susan, you won't believe what happened."

"What?" Susan demanded.

"They want to charge me with neglecting the children
and they took them away from me because I did not clean up
the house."

"You're kidding. Can you believe that shit. I don't
understand. What's next?" said Susan.

"I have to get a lawyer."

"You can't afford a lawyer; do you have any idea what
that would cost?"

"Absolutely. I guess they will appoint some know-noth-
ing from Legal Aid ... someone who barely got through law
school. And he's going to defend me? But, Susan, the best
was when the judge said, 'next time you come into my courtroom, dress appropriately.' And you should have seen how she
looked ... no way she could make a fashion statement ... no

makeup, hair pulled back so tightly into a bun that her cheeks were indented ... couple of curly strands hanging out."

"Can you believe that shit. I will call you later; my mother is ragging on me."

"Okay; later."

CHAPTER 26

———◆———

AFTER THE NEGLECT HEARING, Samantha received a
letter from Legal Aid in Monticello, telling her the time
and place to meet her court-appointed attorney John Rainer.

Samantha daydreamed about what kind of attorney
she would get. I bet it will be some bozo who just about got
through law school. She crumpled up the letter and threw it
into the waste basket.

The next morning, she called Legal Aid.

"Hi, my name is Samantha Jones. I received a letter asking me to call for an appointment with John Rainer."

The receptionist paused, then said,

"How about tomorrow at 10 a.m.?"

"That's great!"

The next morning Samantha drove to Monticello and
did a mental replay of the visit from Social Services, deter-
mining the questions she wanted to ask about the status of her
children. As she entered the lobby, she scanned the building
directory, looking for Legal Aid. She made her way up to the
third floor, suite 312, opened the office door and was greeted.

"Hello, I am Carol, the receptionist. Samantha Jones?"

Sam nodded.

"Could you follow me into the conference room? May I get you anything?"

"No thanks."

Assuming the man entering the conferance room was her court-appointed attorney, Samantha stood and extended her hand.

"I'm Samantha Jones; call me Sam."

"Nice to meet you, Sam. My name is John Rainer."

He pulled out a chair for her and sat down across placing a yellow legal pad and pen on the table.

Sam stared at John trying to place where she might have met him.

"You look like someone I know," she said.

John ignored the comment. Samantha continued to look John over thinking,

"Boy, he actually looks like an attorney; definitely not a bozo."

After some small talk, John said, "Let's get down to business. "Tell me about Samantha," he started.

"What do you mean?"

"Well, where were you born?"

"Livingston Manor."

"Do you have any brothers or sisters?"

"Yes, four sisters and a brother who was adopted by another family way before I was born. They don't talk about him," Samantha explained.

"Do your parents live in Sullivan County?"

"Yes."

"Are you married?"

"No."

Samantha absentmindedly started tapping on the table and became visibly upset with the line of questioning. Eventually she said,

"Stop. I am here for legal advice, not for a psychological evaluation."

John chuckled and explained the need for the information. Samantha's face reflected skepticism, but she decided to cooperate.

"What about school?"

"I quit at 16."

"How old are your children?"

"Soon they will be one year old."

"They are twins?"

John started going down another path of questioning.

"Why did you leave home?"

"None of your business."

"Come on, Sam, cooperate. Help me out here."

He could see her struggling with the answer.

After a pause she spoke,

"They threw me out."

"Why?"

Samantha strained to answer. "My father said if I was old enough to have a baby then I was old enough to live on my own."

"What about your mother?"

"She tried to get my dad to let me stay at home, but he said no."

John could see the tears running down Samantha's

cheeks and gave her a tissue. She nodded and then said with discomfort,

"Can we move on?"

"Okay. So where did you live after you left your parents?"

"An aunt took me in until I had the babies. When they were a few months old I found an apartment through the Salvation Army."

"How about your sisters; couldn't they help?"

"They still live at the house under my father's rule. There is very little they can do to help me. On occasion they send me money when they can for expenses or for baby supplies. But the way I feel about it is simple. These are my children, and this is my problem."

John was impressed with Samantha's tenacity and sense of responsibility.

"How do you get money to live?"

"I hooked up on occasion with a local drunk who offered to help with expenses. When he was not drinking he was okay. But when he drank, he made me his punching bag for his failures in life. After a few times like that, I threw him out," Sam confided, aware that it might not be good to confess this, but she was trying to show that she was a do-whatever-it-takes person.

"That doesn't sound good, Sam. Did you try getting help from Social Services?"

"Yes. They gave me food stamps and W.I.C. for the kids and offered to put me up in a motel. I guess they do this for anyone who has no place to live. I didn't tell them about the guy. Anyway, why would I leave the apartment building on Academy Street? The people who live in the motel, called

The Golden Motel, are mostly child molesters or parolees. ('Golden' ... God, what a stupid name for it ... what's golden about it?)

"I'll tell you, I try to avoid Social Services because they get too nosey," Samantha said, on a roll now.

"Even your caseworker?"

"She couldn't care less. You can never reach her on the phone and if you leave a message, she never calls you back."

"Hmmm. How is your health, Samantha?"

"I take pills for depression when I can get them. But I didn't fill out the papers correctly so I don't have medical coverage."

"What did the case worker say?"

"I couldn't reach her. I told you what happens. It's just too frustrating."

"How about medical care for the girls?"

"I use the emergency room."

"Let's talk about the apartment. How do you manage?"

"Well, I was living with this other guy, not the drunk, who kept saying how much he loved me. I didn't believe him, but he helped pay the expenses. I think the reason he stayed was the occasional sex. It wasn't bad."

John lowered his head, knowing how it would sound but in sympathy with this young lady who had hit the skids.

She continued,

"After a few months, his cousin moved in and slept on the couch. Everything was going good for two weeks; we got along and all pitched in to get the work done. I started to think he might actually care about me. Then one day when I came back from shopping, I found him doing 'his cousin.' Of course, I said something about it. After that nothing got done in the apartment. They left in a month and took the expense money they owed me with them.

"Next, his friend moved in, but he was a slob. I threw him out. I was getting very depressed with the crop of losers that I was picking up and let everything go to hell."

"That's terrible. What about food and clothing, Samantha?"

"I lost the food stamps; I don't know why. So I used the food pantry and churches. The final straw is the eviction notice. I have been there for months, taking care of my little girls and paying the rent, one way or another. All those ways have failed. I just can't take it anymore."

John let the eviction comment pass, knowing that if she was not house-sharing, there was no way she could pay the expenses.

He proceeded to explain the court charges to Samantha who objected to the word 'neglect.'

"There's no use quibbling about words ... that's what you are being charged with."

After that a glaze came over Samantha's eyes as John went on about the law.

Concerned she could come across to the court as cavalier about her lifestyle and trying to snap her to attention, John said,

"If you are found guilty they could place the children in a foster home and eventually put them up for adoption."

Sam interrupted John and screamed out,

"You have got to be kidding."

It was so loud that Carol came running into the conference room to see what happened. John motioned that everything was okay and continued.

"It only happens in extreme cases," he said without much conviction, but trying to settle Samantha down.

There was a heavy pause.

"One more thing," said John, breaking the silence. "Dress appropriately. The judge is a hard ass about that. I will see you in court for the hearing."

"What does 'appropriate' mean? I didn't dress like a hooker or something. I just had on regular clothes. You should see how the judge dresses."

"Samantha, the judge does not dress to impress you; it's the other way around. 'Appropriate' to her means no shorts, no tank tops, nothing with holes in it. The judge automatically assumes those things mean you are disrespectful."

CHAPTER 27

——⋙ ◆ ⋘——

S AMANTHA HAD DIFFICULTY SLEEPING, because the stakes were so high and she did not trust the court system.

As she fell asleep, she dreamed of Jodi and Angel laughing and playing in the back yard. The sun was shining and the twins were playing together, giggling and calling for her. But it was all a dream.

The alarm went off at 7 a.m. At first, she didn't even hear the sound and just lay there thinking about what was going to happen.

"How would it turn out? Would she get her adorable little girls back?"

After a while she realized the alarm had gone off and said to herself,

"I need to move my butt to be on time at court."

Samantha could not forget John's advice to 'dress appropriately.' She rummaged through the clothes on the floor looking for something to wear and slipped on what appeared to be a clean pair of jeans without holes. She found a blouse, combed her hair and then looked in the mirror saying,

"Now, I am appropriately dressed."

Samantha and John met in the hallway of family court.

"Let's find a place to talk."

As John leaned against the wall of the corridor, Samantha sat on the window sill.

"Nice to see you in clean jeans with no holes, Samantha."

He explained the proceedings and what was going to occur.

"Today, the state will present their evidence supporting their decision to remove the twins. We will present our mitigating circumstances that should be considered and ask for our custody plan. This will include supervised visitation and home health aide services. We will agree that the children remain in custody until progress is made by you."

Samantha objected, but John said,

"There should be no objections at this point. Do as I tell you. I want you to have low expectations. We will do everything to get the children returned, but you need to cooperate. Do you understand?"

"Yes," barked Samantha.

CHAPTER 28

—◄◆►—

"JONES: COURTROOM ONE" the speaker sounded out as they continued to discuss the case.

John said to Samantha, "That's us. Let's go."

They entered the courtroom and took their seats at the table in front of the judge. Sitting on the left side of the court was Anna Frank, Ira Tietz and Roberta Black, each in their designated places, waiting for the judge.

In the last row of the courtroom, once again, was Mr. Rameriz, a researcher from the Albany court.

Samantha leaned over and asked John,

"Who is he? Why is he here? Do you know him?"

"Who?"

"The guy in the back of the room. They call him Rameriz."

"I don't know who he is," replied John as he glanced at the well-dressed man.

Abruptly the court officer called for order. The judge entered and took her seat.

"Call the roll," she instructed.

As Judge Henderson listened to the names she halted the proceeding when it came to Rameriz.

"Mr. Rameriz, what is your interest in the case."

He answered in a modulated, respectful voice, but his strength was clear.

"I am here by order of the High Court in Albany. I am studying family court proceedings."

"Welcome to my court," said Judge Henderson, slightly dubious.

"Let's resume."

The judge turned to Ira Tietz from Social Services and said,

"Present your case, Mr. Tietz."

CHAPTER 29

---◆---

IRA BEGAN. "Miss Jones lives in a Salvation Army supported apartment and has no visible means of income that we can document. In fact, Miss Jones is currently being evicted from her apartment due to her poor behavior which is offensive to all her neighbors. As for food and clothing, Miss Jones is dependent on food banks and churches to feed her family. She has refused food stamps or assistance from Social Services. The children have no medical coverage, so she takes them to the emergency room at Harris, or she is dependent upon friends to break the law by neglecting to charge for her medical exams."

Ira called his first witness Anna Frank. Anna described the deplorable conditions in the apartment, painting Samantha as an arrogant and unconcerned mother who cared little about the children's well-being.

"Where does Miss Jones get money to live?" asked the judge.

"From questionable sources...."

"What are you talking about, Mr. Tietz?"

"We think she engages in prostitution."

John yelled out, "Objection! There is no evidence that supports Mr. Tietz's contention."

"Is that true?" asked the judge.

"We are working on developing the facts."

"Then save it for another day. Let's move on with your case," the judge instructed.

Samantha looked at John and said with a moan,

"Could it get any worse? And they are not telling the truth."

John patted her hand. Finally, Anna told the court how she was assaulted by Samantha and required the assistance of the Liberty Police to remove the children.

Judge Henderson scowled over her spectacles and interjected,

"Miss Jones, that is not how a responsible person behaves. Disrespecting authority was not tolerated then and it will definitely not be tolerated in the court. Is that clear?"

"Yes, mam," Samantha softly answered as she looked down at the floor.

"I was just fighting to keep my children."

Ira then concluded his evidence by declaring,

"This woman is unfit to be a parent. We recommend that the children remain in custodial care until the matter is resolved, with no parental visitation."

CHAPTER 30

———◆———

"YOU'RE UP, MS. BLACK," SAID THE JUDGE.
"According to our investigation these two little girls have not had any documented visits to a doctor, and they may be undernourished."

"Have you had the children examined by a doctor, Miss Jones?" asked Judge Henderson.

"No. But the way all of this sounds is not true!" Samantha pleaded.

Ms. Black continued,

"This report was made by the foster home. A preliminary evaluation from Social Services shows the children to be developmentally behind in weight and motor skills."

Samantha yelled out, "no, no!!"

The judge ignored her outburst and instructed John to caution his client. Judge Henderson then turned to John saying,

"It's your turn, Mr. Rainer."

John began explaining Samantha's background and that she had been on her own since sixteen years of age.

"Where are her parents? How come they are not in court?"

"They disowned her when she became pregnant."

"How old are you Samantha?"

"I just turned 18 years old." ('Some birthday party,' Sam thought to herself, her lip quivering.)

It occurred to John that she was just a child herself. He continued, explaining that Samantha had been diagnosed with bouts of depression.

"She has received only limited assistance from Social Services."

"Why," asked Judge Henderson?

"She did not understand how to fill out the paperwork."

Ira interrupted,

"Your Honor, according to our records Miss Jones has not been cooperative and refused all assistance."

The judge halted the proceeding and said,

"Mr. Rainer, do you have any evidence that will refute the claims by Social Services or the attorney for the children?"

"No."

"Then you're done. Let's not waste the court's time."

"I object."

"Your objection is overruled."

"Your Honor, it's important for you to hear the mitigating factors to understand the complete picture."

"Mr. Rainer, sit down. We are discussing facts. You either have them or you don't. Ten-minute recess."

As the court emptied, Samantha just sat motionless in shock.

John said,

"Low expectations."

He explained that he did not have anything to refute the evidence presented by Social Services or the attorney for the children.

"We have to wait until the trial. I need to show that Social Services did nothing to assist you. I need to prove they did nothing to change your living conditions ... but they could have."

CHAPTER 31

———⟡———

JUDGE HENDERSEN ADDRESSED SAMANTHA when she returned and court was called to order.

"Miss Jones, based upon the evidence presented, I find sufficient grounds to continue custodial care. I am setting a trial date for two weeks from today. I would also like you to have a mental health evaluation and be drug tested."

Samantha started crying.

The judge, looking at her, said without compassion,

"You should have thought about the consequences of your actions before you started down this slippery slope."

John and Samantha were taken aback by the judge's harsh remarks.

"What does this mean," asked Samantha.

"You have to trust me and remain calm. You can't show emotion," John said, but admitted,

"At least she could have listened to our side of the story."

"That's for sure," agreed Samantha.

"The judge had no interest in hearing our case or the mitigating facts. We must go forward with even more care. The next time you appear in court, try wearing a dress."

CHAPTER 32

A
FTER A HEARING IN WHICH JOHN HAD VERY LITTLE
SUCCESS and the points he made seemed to go on deaf
ears, Samantha was losing confidence in him.

"He could have fought harder," she thought.

"What good is having a lawyer when they don't defend
you. All he focused on was reminding me to have low expectations. Well, I have low expectations watching him defend
me, that's for sure. I can't believe this is happening."

As the next scheduled meeting with John Rainer drew
closer Samantha's anxiety became more intense.

"Where are those pills I saved up?"

Samantha yanked out the drawer, grabbed the bottle
then popped four pills into her mouth without looking at the
label.

"Where is my water? Oh hell! I'll take a beer. I better get
ready for my meeting with John. He hates when I am late."

As Samantha got ready, she knew John would be pleased
with her choice of clothes. She took the solid blue dress with
white trim she got from Goodwill out of the closet and placed it

over her head. She then smoothed out the ruffles with her hands. After putting on the dress Samantha looked into the mirror.

"Wow. I forgot what it was like to wear a dress."

She then ran a comb through her hair. Just before she left for the meeting with John, she again looked into the mirror and gave herself a thumbs up. But the truth was she was scared to death. Samantha looked at the clock, then hurried to meet John at 9 a.m.

As Samantha arrived at family court, the court officer ushered her to the back office conference room. John was waiting for Sam to arrive. As he looked up, he saw her standing in the doorway smiling.

"Very nice."

But the look on his face told another story. He thought of how she was trying to do this one right thing. Yet it was so imbalanced with the many wrong things that brought her to this point. His heart cried for her.

Samantha joked,

"Your first case?"

John laughed and removed papers from his briefcase.

On the top of the first page were the words 'Mental Health Evaluation.' John read the report and said,

"It looks good."

"And how about the drug test?" asked Samantha.

John noticed a trace of apprehension.

"No evidence of opiates in the blood. Should there be?"

"No," said Samantha, just a little too strongly.

John raised his eyebrows slightly, then moved on.

"The state has a strong case, but not a case that warrants the loss of parental rights. We can prove to the court that the condition of the apartment and your inability to get medical assistance for the children as well as for yourself are connected. Social Services had a responsibility to make sure your depression medication was supplied. It was not. That caused you to tire and lose motivation. And that was the cause of your inability to properly function. Until just recently, you were not even of legal adult age yourself. Social Services did not do their job."

"Does that qualify them to take my children?"

"No, but they can make it difficult for you to get them back. It could take time."

"How much time?" she asked John, her brow furrowed with worry.

"We will have to wait and see. So what do we have? We have mitigating circumstances on our side. We can prove that with services and treatment you could be a responsible parent for the children. We also need to show that you are dealing with your depression responsibly and it will not affect the care of your children.

"Social Services and the Child Advocate attorney will bring up everything they can to prove you are unfit. And don't be surprised if they bring up the prostitution charge, Samantha."

"It's not like I did anything. I stood on the corner making believe for a friend. We would have taken the money and ran. But it didn't happen. And they did not charge me with anything."

"Young lady, you act like these things have no consequences, but they do as you can see," John admonished.

Samantha was quiet, thinking about the seriousness of the situation.

"We must convince the court that you can be a responsible adult and take care of the children."

"I can." said Samantha with conviction."

"When I suggest as part of the custodial plan that you take parenting classes and have a home health aide to assist you, do not blurt out any objections. Do you understand?"

"Yes. All right. I get it. I get it."

"We are going to try to get Social Services' cooperation in getting you housing and medical benefits."

Samantha started to object, thinking of the 'un-Golden' motel, but John put up his hand and said,

"Stop. That's what I'm talking about. You may not blurt out any objections."

John could see the fear in Samantha's face. The children were her whole life and he did not want her to lose them now that he was learning more about Sam and her character. The stakes were never higher than they were today.

"We need to go."

CHAPTER 33

———◆———

As John and Samantha walked through the building towards Courtroom One, the hallway seemed like a long tunnel that never ended. Each step required greater effort and it felt like a force field was preventing them from proceeding.

As they approached, the court officer opened the door and said,

"Take the same seats as you had before."

The court room atmosphere was tense; you could hear a pin drop. The attorneys for each side were making small talk in muffled voices awaiting the arrival of the judge. Samantha could feel the tension and she was sweating profusely. The court officer called for order and read the roll.

Judge Henderson entered, her black robes flowing, her spectacles riding on her nose, a look of no nonsense on her face. She wasted no time, turning to Social Services and saying,

"Present your case, Mr. Tietz."

CHAPTER 34

—◆—

IRA WAS A SHORT STOCKY MAN and his taste in clothes only highlighted his weak points -- his belly hung over his belt and his shirt was barely buttoned. However, as a prosecutor he was fierce and very skilled in cross examining witnesses. Ira's critics described him as heartless with little compassion for those less fortunate. He called his first witness -- Anna Frank.

"Good morning, Ms. Frank. Please tell the court how this young woman, Miss Jones, lives."

Anna began. "Her living conditions are deplorable. Filth, cockroaches, clutter."

"Were the children exposed to unhealthy conditions?"

"Yes, they were. When I went to their room, they were sleeping. Five roaches skittered across as I opened the door. Five. I counted them.

"The apartment is on Academy Street in Liberty and funded by the Salvation Army, but Miss Jones is responsible for all of her operating costs."

"So how does she make ends meet?"

"According to our investigation, Miss Jones allows any man who can help pay her expenses to live in the apartment."

"Would you say all the men are reputable?"

"No. They include ex-convicts, dope heads, drunks and the like."

"Were the children living and interacting with these derelicts?"

"Yes, most of the time."

"How did Miss Jones get money to cover food expenses?"

"Most of it came from food banks."

"Did she have a job?"

"No."

"Let's go back to how Miss Jones got money for her housing expenses. Did she have a roommate?"

"Yes, if you call her drinking buddies roommates. She would let people stay in the apartment and charge them a fee."

"Were the people male or female?"

"Mostly males shared the apartment with her."

"Would you say Samantha is now homeless?"

"Yes."

"Why?"

"Because she is being evicted, with no place to go."

"How about clothing?"

"Miss Jones gets the majority of clothes from the Salvation Army and Goodwill."

"You said 'the majority.' What about the rest?"

"She relies on the churches."

"Does Miss Jones have any medical coverage for herself or the children?"

"No."

"Did Miss Jones refuse medical care from Social Services?"

"Yes."

"Ms. Frank, would you say Samantha Jones is unable to take care of herself or her children?"

"In my opinion, yes!"

"No surprises so far," said John to Samantha.

Ira approached the bench and whispered to the judge. The judge then motioned for John to approach.

Ira spoke,

"Your Honor, I would like to present to the court an affidavit from an undercover policeman in Liberty, stating that Samantha was involved in selling drugs in the Monticello area."

John immediately interjected,

"I strongly object to the submission of the affidavit on the grounds that the person making the statement is not available for cross-examination."

Ira looked at John with disdain as he defended the affidavit,

"The words of the undercover policemen should be considered and validated by his position."

The judge agreed that the information could not be challenged by John because the undercover officer could not be present and, therefore, the affidavit would not be allowed in the court proceedings.

But in a strange turn of events as the lawyers were taking their seats the judge announced to the court and by so doing, entered on the record,

"There is evidence by the Liberty Police that Samantha

was involved in drugs. However, the undercover officer could not attend the proceeding."

John started yelling at the judge,

"We agreed that the information could not be challenged by the defense and is not admissible. I want the record stricken."

"I see your concern; however, it is true that the undercover officer would testify if he were available."

"This is outrageous. You are allowing evidence to be entered into the record that is not admissible."

"No. I am merely reflecting in the record an event that is pertinent."

"You can't do that!!!"

"I can, I will and I just did. Take it up on appeal."

"You know that's not possible," said John. He was still fuming because the damage was done by the actions of the judge.

"Why was the judge not impartial? What was the judge's motivation?" John pondered.

Both Samantha and John were very disappointed.

INTERLUDE

DEMOLISHED CAR UNCOVERED ON THE HUDSON RIVER CLIFFS

Peekskill NY (AP). At dawn today the weather cleared after a particularly dense fog. Route 6 East approach from the Bear Mountain Bridge is said to be the most twisty, serpentine windy road, and it is on the edge of a mountain cliff overlooking the Hudson River. Locals have dubbed it "The Goat Trail." As they gazed from the lookout point, a boy scout troop excitedly announced their discovery – a demolished car that had stopped just above the river's edge after crashing down the rocks.

The car speed before plunging out of control over the cliffside was estimated to have reached 100 mph. The brakes appear to have been faulty. The driver was crushed between the dash board and the roof of the car.

The identity of the deceased is being investigated and the name will be withheld pending notification of the family.

CHAPTER 35

———◆———

JOHN RAINER STARTED HIS CROSS examination of Anna Frank.

"How long have you known Miss Jones?"

"Not very long."

"How long would you say."

"A few months."

"Did you have an opinion of Miss Jones before you met her?"

"Yes."

"What was it?"

"She was irresponsible -- an alcoholic -- and she had questionable sexual behavior."

"How did you arrive at that conclusion?"

"What I heard on the street."

"Had you met her before you went to the apartment?"

"No."

"So you made up your mind before you visited her apartment."

"I guess so. It was obvious what was going on with this woman."

"Really. What was her apartment like?"

"Absolutely despicable."

"Did she give you any explanation for the conditions?"

"Yes. She said she was ill."

"Did you believe her?"

"No."

"Could she have been telling the truth?"

"I doubt it," said Anna.

"Was Samantha ever in Social Services' care?"

"Based upon our records I would say yes."

"What services did you provide to her?"

"We offered her a place to live with the children."

"Where was it?"

"At the nearby motel."

"Isn't true that the motel houses mostly ex-criminals or sexual molesters?"

"Yes."

"Did you consider this motel suitable for young children?"

"Yes."

"Ms. Frank, are you serious?"

"Well, it's all we have."

"Would you place your family in the motel?"

"No."

"Ms. Frank, did Miss Jones have her own apartment? Was the apartment house full of criminals?"

"No."

"Would you say her current apartment was more suitable?"

Anna paused then said, "Yes."

"So why could she not stay in her apartment?"

"It was not on our approved list of places."

"Did you provide her with food stamps and W.I.C. for the girls?"

"Yes."

"Isn't it true you took the food stamps away?"

"Yes."

"Why?"

"She did not complete her application for renewal."

"Did anyone *provide* any assistance to her in completing the forms?"

"I don't know."

"So what did you do to help her?"

"We gave her access to services and she did not use them."

"How about medical care? Why didn't Miss Jones and the two little girls have Medicaid?"

"She refused it!"

"Why?"

"I don't know."

"Do you think her caseworker should have followed up?"

"I guess so."

"Did the caseworker know she had depression?"

"No."

"Why was it not in the file?"

"I don't know."

"So you left the 17-year-old Miss Jones and the year-old twins to fend for themselves knowing she was ill."

"We can't follow-up on everyone. We need the consumer's help."

"So let's recap: You gave her a choice to either live with child molesters or stay in her apartment without services. You provided her with no food stamps, and she had no medical care for herself or the twins. Now you want to remove the children from her custody because she is unable to care for them according to Social Services. Yet you are the ones who took away her ability to get treated or have her children receive medical care.

"I am truly amazed by your compassion for her plight." John sarcastically commented, then he sat down.

"Points on the board," Samantha whispered.

Chapter 36

———◆———

Ira called his next witness Roberta Black.

"Ms. Black, what do you do?"

"I am the attorney for the children."

"How are the children?"

"They are doing just fine. They are adjusting to foster care."

"What about their physical condition?"

"They have gained weight and are playing with other children."

"Are there any concerns?"

"Yes. The doctor expressed concern for their well-being."

"What do you mean?" said Ira.

"He felt the previous environment was not suitable for the children."

"You mean the house they were living in at the time they were removed."

"Yes."

"No more questions," said Ira.

Chapter 37

———◆———

JOHN ROSE FROM HIS CHAIR and stood in front of Ms. Black.

"When the children came into your custody, were they sickly?"

"I don't think so."

"Did they have lice, ticks or fleas."

"I don't know."

"Did they have bug bites on their body?"

"I don't know."

"How would you compare the girls to other children you have come into contact with during your tenure as a guardian ad litem attorney?"

"They were in good health despite not having access to medical care."

"Ms. Black, when was the last time you saw the children?"

"I only talked to the foster parent."

"So how do you know how the children are?"

"I asked Wanda."

"You claim the children were seen by a doctor."

"Yes."

"Did he give them shots?"

"I don't know."

"Did he find anything wrong with the children?"

"I don't know."

"What did he treat them for?"

"I don't know."

"So we must conclude you really don't know much about the well-being of the children. You are basing all your information on the foster parent that you have not even met. I am finished with her," said John.

CHAPTER 38

❖

JOHN PRESENTED HIS CASE.

"I will agree with Social Services that Miss Jones must take full responsibility for the children and their environment. However, I would like to remind the court of her tragic past and her living without parental guidance for a number of years. Despite the lack of housing and medical services, Miss Jones and the children have survived. What would their life be had they had been handled properly by Social Services? I would expect it would be significantly better. Some would say she would not be in this court today.

"Social Services was well aware that Miss Jones had been diagnosed with psychotic depression, which covers depressed mood, appetite changes and loss of interest in all her activities. In extreme cases, she could have hallucinations and delusions. So how can this young woman control her disease if she cannot receive treatment and obtain medicine? Without medical treatment or money for medicine she has no hope of managing the depression. As to her refusing medical care, her state of depression would certainly contribute to the irrational decision. It looks to me like we were setting her up to fail by withholding services. Now we want to punish her by taking away her children? Your Honor, this is a very sad story."

John felt good. He had presented a case in which mitigating factors could play a role in the final decision as to what would happen with the children.

The judge then asked,

"Mr. Tietz, do you have any other comments?"

"No, Your Honor."

"Mr. Rainer, do you have any more information you would like to share with the court?"

"Yes, Your Honor."

CHAPTER 39

————◆————

"I WOULD LIKE TO PROPOSE AN ALTERNATIVE to removing the children from Miss Jones's custody. Under our plan the children would remain in custodial care. Miss Jones would be required to seek medical care for her depression under the supervision of Social Services. She would be required to obtain parenting skills and receive treatment for her drinking. Social Services would work with her to find a new apartment, provide her with food stamps and have a home health aide assist her with managing the apartment.

"As Miss Jones's condition improves she would be granted supervised visitation. Over time the visitation would include visits in her home."

The judge acknowledged John's plan but had no comment.

CHAPTER 40

———◆———

IRA ADDRESSED THE COURT. "Your Honor, considering the implications of Mr. Rainer's proposal, we need more information. I call Miss Samantha Jones to the stand."

As she rose, the sweat beads on her brow were clearly visible. John watched with great intensity as she took a seat in the witness box.

Ira said to Samantha,

"I only have a few questions for you. Tell me Miss Jones, why did you leave your home?"

"I got pregnant and my father asked me to leave his house."

"Did the boy offer to marry you?"

"No."

"Did you want him to marry you?"

"At first I did, then I didn't."

"Does the young man want anything to do with the twins?"

"No."

"Why not?"

"Because he says he does not know if they're his."

"Did you offer to get a paternity test?"

"No. I told him it was my first time."

"I guess he didn't believe you."

"Objection Your Honor," John interjected.

"Sustained."

"Why didn't you get an abortion?" Ira continued.

"I refused to kill my babies."

"Why didn't you put them up for adoption?"

"They are *my* children."

"Are you religious?"

"Yes, I am Christian?"

"Do you go to church?"

"Sometimes."

"Why didn't you go to live with your sisters after the children were born?"

"My sisters are still living with my father so there is very little they can do for me."

"Since you lived with your aunt for a while, why didn't you continue to stay there after your children were born?"

"I wanted to be the mother of my children on my own. My aunt understood being independent is important to me and told me about the Salvation Army apartments, so I went and got one."

"When you were under the care of Social Services did you tell them about the depression?"

"Yes, I think so."

"You either did or you did not tell them."

"I did."

"How about your caseworker? Did you tell her?"

"Yes, I did. But she said everybody gets depressed and blew it off."

"Why didn't you go to the motel that Social Services told you about so they could attend to all your needs including housing?"

"I already had an apartment, so why leave it. And why would I expose my children to pedophiles and people like that?"

"Did you tell the case worker about your concerns?"

"Yes."

"What did she say?"

"Everybody has hard times."

"Did the social worker follow-up with you?"

"No."

"Why?"

"No offense, but how would I know? I would call her and she would not call me back."

"Why didn't you go to her office?"

"I couldn't because I did not have transportation at the time."

"How did you get around?"

"Friends. If they were going somewhere I would ask them if I could hitch a ride to the same place, but I didn't get a ride to somewhere they were not going."

"Do you think the environment you have for the children is a healthy one?"

"It is better than the motel. In fact my transportation is better now too cause my best friend gave me an old truck. I was hoping I could improve my life. See; I just need a little help. I was hoping I could improve my life. I just need help."

"What about the men in your life?"

"What do you mean?"

Ira raised his voice.

"Why are you sleeping with every street person in Liberty?"

Samantha dropped her head in shame.

"Your Honor, I strongly object. What a ridiculous accusation!" John burst out.

"Sustained. Mr. Tietz, you know better than to generalize like that."

Ira paused briefly, then turned and said,

"I'll rephrase the question. What about your prostitution charge?"

Before Samantha could answer Ira interrupted,

"Never mind," intending to do the damage before John could object and remove the stain from the record.

CHAPTER 41

—◆—

JOHN WAS ONTO IRA's strategy and would not let the image
remain without their side having a say. He called Samantha to the stand.

"Miss Jones, are you sleeping with every street person
in Liberty?"

"No."

"What about the prostitution charge?"

"I was standing on the corner when the police arrested
me."

"What did they charge you with?"

"Loitering. Then even that charge was dropped."

"Not prostitution?"

"That's right."

John was concerned about the expression on the judge's
face when she asked,

"Have you finished your case, Mr. Rainer?"

"Yes, Your Honor. We rest."

"Mr. Tietz, are you finished?"

"Yes, Your Honor."

"Then we will take a 10-minute recess. When I come back I will hear your summations and render a decision."

CHAPTER 42

———◆———

A S JOHN AND SAMANTHA LEFT the courtroom they both felt good. They had presented a good case, refuted the issues brought up by Social Services and provided alternatives to removing the children from their mother. It made good sense.

After Judge Henderson returned to the bench, court reconvened.

"Mr. Tietz, your summary please."

"Your Honor, Samantha Jones represents a tragic story about a young woman gone wrong. She has shown her inability to deal with her medical issues and has not made any progress in dealing with her drinking or depression. As for the children, we have heard the testimony of their guardian ad litem attorney regarding the health and welfare of the children. Miss Jones is on the verge of losing her apartment and could be homeless. Even with services we believe that Miss Jones is incapable of taking care of the children. We therefore ask the children be remanded to foster care permanently."

"Mr. Rainer, your summary."

"Mr. Tietz is correct, this is a tragic case. Miss Jones' parents failed her and the system failed her. Taking away her children and placing them into permanent custodial care would be another failure she would have to suffer.

"There has been no effort by Social Services to bring this young family together. We have given to the court a plan to reunite the children with their mother and ensure that her problems are addressed and monitored by Social Services."

"Thank you, Mr. Rainer."

"Miss Jones, do you have anything to say to the court?"

"Yes, Judge. I have always tried to be a good mother. I have never done anything to hurt my children and have made sure they had something to eat, a place to live and clothes. I can see the errors of my ways and I now know what I need to do to fix things. I hope you will give my children back to me and let me be their mother and give them a new life with me. Please," Samantha implored.

As Samantha sat down John Rainer patted her hand and said,

"Good job."

"Miss Jones, it is tragic that you chose to follow such a course. After listening to and reviewing all of the evidence I must conclude that your issues of depression, coupled with irresponsible behavior and drinking make you an unfit mother. The children will continue in foster care with the oversight of the guardian ad litem attorney and social services."

John and Samantha were stunned by the decision.

"Your Honor, this is unfair!"

"Mr. Rainer, sit down," Judge Henderson ordered.

"I want to appeal!"

"You have no grounds."

"What you're doing is wrong."

"Be careful, Mr. Rainer. You're treading on dangerous ground."

"At least give us an explanation for your decision, Your Honor."

"Mr. Rainer, I don't have to give any explanation for my decision."

Meanwhile Samantha lay her head on the table and sobbed.

"I want to die! I want to die!"

As the judge was leaving the courtroom, she stopped, turned, and with a cold, callous expression on her face, spoke to Samantha,

"You should have thought about what you were doing long before, Miss Jones. Your behavior was nothing but a downhill slide."

Samantha seemed paralyzed as she slumped.

"Mr. Rameriz, please assist Mr. Rainer with walking out Miss Jones," the judge instructed.

As they half dragged, half walked Samantha from the courtroom, Rameriz said to John,

"We need to talk."

CHAPTER 43

———◆———

OUTSIDE OF THE COURTROOM when Rameriz had an opportunity to talk with John he shared his perspective.

"A real tough case. I thought the Judge would have gone for the alternative plan. It looked like her mind was made up before she rendered a decision."

"Be careful with that type of accusation," said John.

Rameriz raised his eyebrows,

"Let's have lunch."

"Okay," John agreed, wondering if this were part of Rameriz' research.

Samantha had made arrangements for her friend Susan to pick her up. She continued to sob while she waited for her ride.

Chapter 44

IRA HAD A MEETING WITH THE JUDGE on Monday morning.

"Good morning, Judge."

"Did you bring me coffee?"

"Yes. I also got you a bagel with cream cheese."

"Thanks. You're so sweet, Ira."

"That was a tough scene in court. John was very upset with the decision."

"That's too bad."

"What is our next move on the Jones' case?" asked Ira.

"Permanently removing the twins and immediately placing them up for adoption. How fast can we move?"

"I will have Sol draw up the papers. What is his cut?"

"It's 10%. Let's get back to Miss Jones. We need more evidence to prove her unfit."

"Like what?"

"The prostitution charge."

"They only issued a citation then changed it to loitering, and even that was dropped," Ira answered defensively.

"So what? Let's blow it up to a crime against humanity. Do you know what I mean?"

"Yes," said Ira. "Drugs?"

"I want you to prove she is affecting young children or selling in school. Talk to the undercover cop. Frame her if necessary. Who is going to be concerned about a street urchin."

"You know that John will be a problem."

"Why?" said Colleen.

"He does not believe that removing the children was warranted."

"Obviously. But who cares? I am the judge. There is no appeal. I will meet with him and try to smooth out his feathers."

Ira cautioned, "Okay, but be careful. He is not trustworthy and won't play ball,"

"He does not have to agree with us. He needs to do his job – present the case as he sees it and that's it – no overzealousness."

"By the way, what is Wanda's cut?"

"Why do you ask? The standard 3%."

"Well, Wanda phoned me last night and demanded a bigger cut 'or else.'"

"She is becoming a real bitch; always about 'poor me.' I thought you talked to her about this before."

"I did! She wants more."

"Don't we all. How much more?" Colleen asked Ira.

"An additional 4%."

"Bullshit," responded Colleen with a snarl.

"She is getting very greedy. Tell her no, Ira. If she continues to be a problem it will be a time for a change.... Do you understand, Ira?"

"Yes, I do. Oh, have you heard the rumor?"

"What rumor?" asked Colleen with a sharp stare at Ira.

"There is an investigation regarding excessive placements by the court."

"Who is the investigator?"

"No one knows."

"I don't believe a word," pooh-poohed Colleen.

"Just water fountain gossip. I will set up a meeting with Wanda for next week. And I will see you later in the court. Ira, in the meantime, make a call to your contacts in Albany and see if they heard anything about the investigation."

"Okay."

CHAPTER 45

───◆───

RAMERIZ AND JOHN MET in the court hallway awaiting the start of another case. Rameriz slapped John on the back,

"How are you doing? That was one tough case."

"Which one?"

"The Jones case."

"It wasn't a tough case; it was a frame up.

"That judge was brutal," agreed Ramirez.

John gazed out the window in deep thought.

"Our plan was workable and a good alternative to splitting up the family. She should not lose her children."

"Will she?"

"Probably," John quietly responded.

"Can you do anything for her?"

"No, not really."

"How many children got placed for adoption this year?"

"A lot more since Judge Henderson took the bench."

"Why is that?"

"I don't know," said John.

CHAPTER 46

———◆———

COLLEEN PLACED A CAL TO SOL, an attorney who represented the Mafia family in New York City and maintained a private practice specializing in private adoptions.

"Hi Sol. How are you?"

"Fine. Why the call?"

"We have a small problem."

"What is it?"

"Wanda is threatening to expose the plan to the authorities."

"Really. What is her issue?"

"More money, but it's only the start with her."

"Did Ira talk to her?"

"Yes. She gave us two weeks … or else."

"Don't get too upset, because she is not ready to go to jail."

"What is our alternative?"

"You don't want to know on the phone. When are you planning to come to New York City, Colleen?"

"Next week."

"Let's make plans to meet."

"Sol, we need to move fast."

"Don't worry, I will take care of it quickly. I have contacted a number of clients who are ready to adopt the Jones twins. The price is getting higher. The top bid that we have is $100,000. I think we should be able to get at least $125,000."

"That's great."

CHAPTER 47

---◆---

SAMANTHA DIALED SUSAN'S PHONE and waited for her to pick up. As Susan answered she could hear a frail voice saying,

"Susan I am in trouble."

"What's wrong?"

"I am having hallucinations. Sometimes I see myself jumping off a cliff with the children. I am terrified."

"Do you want me to call for help?"

"No. Come and take me to Harris."

"I'll be there in 10 minutes. Just hang on."

"Okay," Samantha hung up the phone.

Susan arrived at the apartment within minutes and found the front door wide open. She yelled out,

"Sam, where are you?"

She called out again. There was no response.

"Samantha! Answer me, damn it!"

Susan walked into the bedroom where she found Samantha spread eagled on the floor half naked. She shook her several times but Sam was unresponsive.

"You dumb bitch. Wake up!"

Susan pleaded with feigned irritation with the girl who had been her long term friend. She looked around the room and saw an empty pill bottle marked 'antidepressant.' She read the label on the bottle: 'Do not take with alcohol.' On the floor Susan observed several beer bottles, and there were pills spread over the kitchen counter top. She shook Samantha's unresponsive body and yelled,

"Wake up!"

Samantha remained unresponsive, hardly breathing.

Susan wasted no time and immediately called the Liberty Police.

"Please send an ambulance to 122 Academy Street, Apartment 2. My friend is unconscious."

"What happened?" the police dispatcher asked.

"I don't know. But I do know she suffers from depression and she drinks. She called me and said she was in trouble."

Minutes later Susan heard the police sirens in the background. Then the Liberty Police entered the downstairs hallway door and banged on the front door of the apartment. Susan opened the it and they entered. They immediately started questioning Susan.

"Who are you?"

"I am a friend of Samantha."

"Where is she?"

Susan pointed to the bedroom. As they entered the room they immediately called the dispatcher to rush the ambulance then returned to questioning Susan.

"Are there any drugs in the house?"

"I don't know."

"Does she do drugs?"

"Not that I know of."

"Does she take medicine for any illness?"

"Yes. She has depression."

Susan handed the open pill bottle to the policemen.

"Any other medicine in the house?"

"I don't know. I didn't check the closets."

Just as she finished talking to the police the EMTs made their way into the apartment. They opened the gurney and placed Samantha on it then attached her to the heart monitor.

She was barely breathing so they placed an oxygen mask over her nose, took her pulse and monitored her heart. They tried to wake her without success. After some discussion as to the cause, they covered her with blankets and transported her to Harris Hospital.

CHAPTER 48

———◆———

As THE AMBULANCE PULLED into emergency parking at Harris, standing outside were two nurses and a doctor. Samantha was transported inside and placed on an IV.

Dr. Sullivan introduced herself to Susan and asked, "Can you tell me what happened?"

"The only thing I know is she suffers from depression."

After a few hours and several tests Dr. Sullivan admitted Samantha to ICU. Her condition vascillated throughout the night. Twice the nurses almost lost her.

The next morning the nurse shook her.

"Samantha wake up."

She opened her eyes,

"Where am I?"

"You're at Harris Hospital."

"What happened?"

"We were hoping you could tell us," said the nurse.

Later in the morning, Dr. Sullivan came in to see her.

"You had us worried last night. We are going to conduct a few more tests today and if the results are satisfactory we will transfer you to the main floor."

The next morning Dr. Sullivan told Samantha the test results were negative.

"We are moving you to the general ward. You should be discharged within the next few days."

As Samantha was being wheeled into her new room the nurse placed her medical file on the gurney while she attended to the IV then left for a replacement bag, leaving the medical file behind. Samantha opened the file and looked at the diagnoses: *Attempted Suicide.*

She closed the file and leaned back in her bed. Stunned by the finding, Samantha's anxiety went into overdrive wondering what effect this would have on getting her twins back from the court.

During the discharge process Dr. Sullivan provided Samantha with a script for medicine to treat her depression.

After Dr. Sullivan left the room Samantha threw the script into the garbage thinking,

'What a waste.'

Just then the phone rang; it was Susan.

"I'm picking you up at the main entrance of the hospital."

She parked her car in the front of the hospital and while waiting for Samantha to come out, she started reading her mail. She noted a letter from from Peter with the return address of NASA Houston Texas. She tore open the envelope as Samantha jumped into car and quickly placed it under her seat.

"Well good morning Sam; how do you feel?"

"Ok. I just want to go home."

Susan sensed Samantha's needs; there was silence during the trip; she would talk with her friend when she was ready.

CHAPTER 49

UPON ARRIVAL AT HER APARTMENT Samantha picked up the phone and called her attorney.

"Is John available?"

He was out so she left a message.

Later that day, John called her back. "Hi, Sam. What do you need?"

"An appointment."

"How about 9:00 a.m. tomorrow?"

"Ok. That's great."

"See you tomorrow."

As Samantha entered his office, she met John in the hallway.

"Hi Sam. You look like you need more sleep."

"I know. I was in the hospital for a few days. Depression again."

"Are you getting any medical treatment?"

"No."

John's major concern was Samantha's overall appearance. In addition to looking tired, she had bags under her eyes, wrinkled clothing and stains on her blouse and sandals. John escorted her to the conference room. Samantha sat next to him; he could see the strain in her face.

"Samantha, the case is over. There is little we can do to change the judge's decision. An appeal to Albany would not be successful."

She asked in a soft voice,

"What did I do that was so wrong?"

"Nothing."

"Then why do they have my children?"

"I don't know, and I can't explain the reason. Samantha, I will make one more attempt to change the judge's mind but I am not hopeful."

Samantha's face reflected her frustration and disgust with the system. John escorted her to the door then decided, based upon their conversation, to walk her to the car. He put his arms around her and whispered,

"I am sorry."

Samantha acknowledged the hug with a nod. As John walked back to his office he thought about the case and the question Samantha asked him. He sat in his chair, put his face in his hands and said to himself,

"I don't understand the why."

John pulled out the case and started reviewing her file.

"Did I miss anything?"

CHAPTER 50

———◆———

J OHN DECIDED TO CALL THE JUDGE the next morning
and set up an appointment.

"Good morning. Is the judge available?"

"No," said her secretary.

"How is her calendar for today?"

"I have an open time slot for 10 a.m."

"Pencil me in."

"What is the case?"

"Samantha Jones."

As John thought about what he would say to the judge he
clearly understood the slim possibility of changing the view of
the case and her decision. But he needed to try. His main goal
was to stop their adoption.

At 10:00 a.m. John knocked on the judge's door and
entered her office.

"Good morning Your Honor."

"Right on time. What can I do for you, Mr. Rainer?"

"I would like to discuss the Samantha Jones case."

"What is there to discuss?"

"The decision, Your Honor. Why is my alternative plan unacceptable?"

"It isn't the plan, it's the person. Miss Jones is unfit to raise children."

"I realize she has made mistakes Your Honor, but they don't rise to the level of severe neglect."

"Samantha Jones is not salvageable. Let's not pull punches. I intend to accelerate the adoption process. I don't want to talk about her anymore."

"What is the problem? Why can't you give this kid a break? What is it? Are you getting paid to put the children up for adoption?"

John knew he had crossed the line.

"I'm sorry Your Honor."

"Who do you think you are talking to? If you mention such accusations like that to anyone I will have you disbarred. Now get out of my office."

"Placing children up for adoption hit a nerve," thought John.

Regardless, it was clear that Samantha's chances of having the judge reverse her decision were slim and none. He felt bad that he had gotten into an argument with Judge Henderson. But it was over now and there was nothing he could do for Samantha.

CHAPTER 51

—⋙◆⋘—

SAMANTHA CALLED JOHN the next morning. "Did you talk to the judge?"

"Yes"

"What did she say?"

"It wasn't good. She is going to accelerate the adoption process."

"I don't understand!"

"I give you my word I will get to the bottom of this case. I will find out what is driving the judge's attitude."

Samantha hung up the phone. "This is bullshit. I can't believe this is happening to me."

She walked over to the refrigerator, grabbed a beer and sat down in the chair muttering,

"I can't handle this," and chug-a-lugged one beer after another until she fell asleep.

CHAPTER 52

———◆———

SAMANTHA RECEIVED A LETTER from family court the next morning stating: 'The Court hereby orders the permanent removal of Jodi and Angel Jones from the parental custody of Samantha Jones.'

The tears fell from her eyes. "They are taking away my babies."

She continued reading: 'A hearing will be conducted to determine accelerating the adoption….'

"I have lost everything."

The phone rang.

"Who is this?"

"It's Peter. You know who I am."

"What do you want? I told you never to call me."

"I just wanted to see how the girls are."

"You're kidding!"

"I also wanted to see how you are."

"Why? You want a free piece of ass? Go fuck yourself."

As she hung up the phone she thought,

"He has some nerve."

CHAPTER 53

—◆—

JOHN CALLED RAMERIZ. "Let's do lunch."

"Okay. Some place cheap."

"How about the Raceway Diner. It's not fancy but the food is good."

"Fine. See you at one-thirty."

John arrived at the diner early. As he sat waiting for Rameriz he could hardly contain his emotions thinking about Samantha.

Suddenly Rameriz tapped John on the shoulder from behind.

"Have you been waiting long?"

"I just got here," said John, not wanting to disclose how much time he had been there, thinking about Samantha and her kids.

"Let's order first, then we can talk, Rameriz."

The waitress said, "What will you have?"

"I will have a burger, fries, and regular coffee," said Rameriz.

"I'll have the same," said John.

"I understand you were in the Marines, John."

"Yes. First Marine Division."

"That's a west coast division isn't it?"

"Yes, I went to boot-camp at Pendleton. I was born on the east coast and moved to the west coast. After completing two years of college, pre-med, I joined the Marines. My father was a Marine. How about you?"

"Second Marine Division. Boot camp at Parris Island, South Carolina."

"What was your MOS?" asked John.

"After advanced Infantry training school, I was assigned to Drill Instructor school at Parris Island. I spent three years, then I transferred back to the Second Marines Infantry Battalion. How about you?"

"A medic trained by the Navy and assigned to a Marine Battalion," said John.

"When did you become a lawyer?"

"After leaving the Marines I went to work at the VA hospital in Atlanta, GA. Great contacts and I still have many friends at the hospital. But I decided that medicine was not for me. I attended Emory University Law School."

"How did you wind up on the east coast?"

"I met a girl in South Carolina while on vacation, we dated then got married and I decided to move to the east coast. I love family law, and an opening came about in Sullivan County. So here I am."

"But Sullivan County?"

"Let's just say I was on a mission. It gives me a chance to work with people and assist them in life. How about you?"

"I started with family court in Albany and I was promoted to the Chief Justice Office as a researcher."

"So what are you working on now?"

"The psychological effects of placement on children."

"Sounds interesting."

"John, are there any people I should talk to about this research project?"

"Yes, I would start with Social Services. Ira is a weird duck but smart. I would touch base with Anna Frank -- fresh out of graduate school and smart. And if you're looking for a judge, I would recommend Judge Henderson."

"Why?"

"She has the highest number of placements and almost every one was adopted."

"Where did she come from before Sullivan County?"

"I don't know."

"How do you feel about the placement policy?"

"I am for uniting families, not destroying them."

"I hear you," said Rameriz.

CHAPTER 54

———◆———

B ACK AT HIS OFFICE, Rameriz set up an interview schedule for all the parties suggested by John, called each person and confirmed the date and time.

On returning to Family Court, Rameriz ran into Samantha.

"Do you remember me?" she asked him.

"Yes, I have seen you before in court."

"What do you do?"

"I am a researcher for the chief judge in Albany."

"Why are you sitting in on my case?"

"It's interesting."

Samantha rolled her eyes and pinned him down,

"Do you think the judge was unfair?"

"I think the judge should have listened closer to John's argument."

"Can I take that as a yes?"

Rameriz nodded his head and they proceeded with small talk.

Chapter 55

—◆—

Samantha contacted Rameriz at the court with a "What's up?"

"How are you feeling?" said Rameriz.

"Ok. But I just can't get over the actions of the judge. When we last spoke you said that you would give me a contact in Albany that might help me with my case.

"I did say that. Are you sure you want to contact my person in Albany?"

"Yes. Why?"

"Because he is direct and will not pull his punches."

"I am ready to hear whatever he has to say."

"The person you want to speak to is Tom Ashcroft. Tell Tom that I asked you to call him."

"Okay."

CHAPTER 56

———◆———

L ATER THAT DAY, SAMANTHA CALLED TOM and waited
with trepidation as the phone seemed to ring on and on.

"Family Court. May I help you."

"Tom Ashcroft, please."

"Hold on."

"Hello, this is Tom Ashcroft."

"My name is Samantha Jones and Mr. Rameriz told me
to call you."

"How is the old dog? How do you know him?"

"I met him at the Sullivan County Family Court."

"What can I do for you?"

Samantha told Tom the entire story.

"Has there been a final decision?"

"No, the hearing is coming up."

"When the judge issues a final decree, call me."

"Okay."

As she hung up the phone she was encouraged by Tom
Ashcroft's words, but knew better than to rely on any promises.

CHAPTER 57

———◆———

A FTER THE PHONE CALL SAMANTHA BEGAN TO FEEL
a sense of helplessness. Her depression was getting
worse and she did not have many pills left. She kept drinking
and after several beers fell into a deep sleep.

Much later Samantha awoke, got dressed and headed out
to the Purple Onion, a bar in White Lake. As she entered the
bar, she waved to the men playing pool. She pulled out a bar
stool, sat down and ordered a Coors Light from the bartender.

After sitting there for a few minutes, she heard someone
whispering her name.

"Samantha."

She turned. It was Ramirez.

"Buy me a drink?"

As she looked up at Rameriz she noticed his pony tail
and beard. "A new look?"

Rameriz was silent.

"You look like a vagrant."

As Samantha continued to talk with Rameriz she drank
one beer after another. Finally, her condition was apparent

with slurring of words and her inability to complete sentences.

"How about I drive you home?"

"Sure. And you can take me to bed."

Rameriz smiled. It didn't take long before they reached her house. Samantha tried to kiss Rameriz, but he gently pushed her away. Lovely and needy as she was, he would not take advantage of her or behave in an unprofessional manner.

"You need to get some sleep. We will talk in the morning."

CHAPTER 58

—◆—

RAMERIZ SAW THE SUNLIGHT through the blinds as he got up to take a shower. Today, he was meeting with Ira Tietz, Anna Frank and Judge Henderson. His agenda was to discuss the pending regulations for the adoption of children held in foster care. But his real goal was to obtain information about adoptions in Sullivan County.

The first meeting started at eleven. Ira was sitting in his office on Community Lane in Liberty. When Rameriz arrived, the guard at the door announced him.

"Ira, you have a person here to see you."

"Does he have a pony tail and beard?"

"Yes."

"Let him in and direct him to the conference room."

As Rameriz entered the room, Ira was sitting in his leather chair. Ira said

"Why don't you get a haircut and shave?"

Rameriz smiled and asked,

"How long have you been with the agency?

"Ten years."

"How long have you known Judge Henderson?"

"Eight years."

"A good jurist?"

"Yes, the best."

"What do you think about the new regulations regarding adoption of foster care children?"

"I haven't read all of the regulations. What are they trying to achieve?"

"Limit the number of children sent to foster homes. They are also trying to keep families together."

"That idea has merit."

"It should make your job easier."

"Maybe."

Out of the blue Ira said to Rameriz:

"Who are you?"

"What do you mean?"

"What are you doing here?"

"What do you mean?"

"I mean that when I called Albany nobody knew who you were."

"Really?"

"They gave me some guy named Tom Ashcroft. He knew you, but he was very vague about what you do."

"Well he's my boss. The problem is he is not very talkative."

"I don't believe that. And another thing -- what's with the name 'Rameriz.' Is that your first or last name?"

"It's my last name."

"So why do you have people use Rameriz as a first name?"

"Well, my mother would say – 'Rameriz do this, Rameriz do that.' So it stuck, the name 'Rameriz.'"

"I feel really uneasy talking to you without resolving my concerns."

"Then call my boss and I will be back."

Rameriz got out of his chair and walked out of the room and down the hallway. He could hear Ira calling Tom Ashcroft. As he reached Anna Frank's cubicle he greeted her.

"Hi."

She smiled, then he said,

"Nice digs. How long have you been with the agency?"

"Three years. I interned for a year."

"Is this what you thought it would be like?"

"Yes and no."

"Have you read the report on foster children and adoption?"

"Yes. I don't know where we're going to get the staffing to supervise all these people. It keeps the family together ... Please ... For how long?"

"It's an alternative to foster care."

"Can you think of any cases that would qualify for this program if it were enacted today?"

"No."

"Well, how about Samantha Jones?"

"You're kidding. She is unfit to supervise any children."

"Why?"

"Because she is just like my mother -- a slut. Do you know how hard I had to work to make it?"

"But you made it."

"Well, those two children are going."

"Where?"

"Forget what I said. We will see what the judge decides."

CHAPTER 59

"I WOULD LIKE TO MEET WITH YOU if it's possible. It's very important," was Rameriz's telephone greeting.

"How about 10:00 a.m.," offered John.

At ten, Rameriz walked into John's office. He was escorted into the conference room by the secretary. John entered and the men shook hands.

"I ran your service record and you are highly decorated. You also have a Top Secret clearance and your background is impeccable."

"Why would you do that? What's going on?"

"What if I told you that I'm not who I appear to be?"

"What are you talking about?"

"John, I am an undercover investigator for the State Police. I am researching illegal adoptions in Sullivan County."

"What are you talking about?"

"We have information that a judge and various highly placed employees in Social Services are running an adoption ring. Children from foster care are illegally sold to private parties. The adoptions are being handled by Sol Bernstein, a New York Attorney."

"How did you trace him to Sullivan County?"

"A New York City Mob Hit Investigation disclosed his name in a wiretap. The information led to Sullivan County."

"So why are you telling me?"

"We need someone inside the court system. Based upon your military service and clearance from the government we thought you could help us. Will you?"

"I don't know. I will try to assist you in the Jones case. But I'm not sure about anything else."

"Let's start there. Our main contact will be Tom Ashcroft in Albany. He is an uncover agent for the FBI."

"How big is this investigation?"

"Statewide. Ira Tietz and Wanda Torres are our prime suspects."

"I don't believe it. What is the evidence?"

"I will discuss that with you later. We also think the Jones case is an illegal adoption case, and that's also why we are interested in you."

"Have you told Samantha?"

"Absolutely not."

"What can I do?" said John out of curiousity.

"At this time just continue your everyday routine. I will contact you when needed."

As Rameriz left, John looked out the window thinking about Samantha.

"How could this go on without anyone discovering it? How could Ira make this happen without a judge? It doesn't make sense," John said to himself.

"Could it be Judge Henderson?"

CHAPTER 60

———◆———

L ATER THAT DAY RAMERIZ CALLED WANDA.
"Is one thirty a good time to meet with you?"

"Yes."

Rameriz drove to Wanda's home in Liberty, knocked on her door and listened for evidence of someone being at home. A short paunchy woman with dark brown eyes answered the door.

"What do you want?"

"It's me -- Rameriz. You said I could come."

"Oh. Come in."

As Rameriz walked through the house he could not help but notice the opulence: a large TV, expensive furniture, paintings on the wall and a diamond ring on her hand that had to be three carats.

"The foster care business must be good," he mumbled.

He looked into the bedroom and spotted Samantha's girls playing.

"Would you like some coffee?"

"No thanks. I've had more than enough today."

As they sat at the table Rameriz asked Wanda,

"What does your husband do?"

"He is disabled and cannot work."

"So how many children do you currently have?"

"Three. One will be returned to his parents and the other two are being adopted."

"What is your role in adoptions?"

"I usually take the children to meet prospective parents at the lawyer's office."

"Which lawyer are we talking about?

"Tom Green or Ben Grossman."

"Do they practice in Sullivan County?"

"No. They have an office in Monticello on Washington Street, but they specialize in adoptions. Their main office is in New York City on Park Avenue. When the children are adopted I deliver them to the lawyer's office."

"Have you ever met the lawyers in person?"

"No. I just hand them over to Sally."

"Who is she?"

"A paralegal for the lawyers."

Wanda was getting nervous.

"Have you read the new proposal on limiting adoptions?"

"No, the judge told me not to waste my time."

"Have you ever met an attorney named Sol Bernstein?"

"No. I've never heard of such a person. Who is he?"

"Just a person of interest," said Rameriz.

"How long have you been a foster parent?"

"Seven years."

"Let me explain the new regulations. The children would not be sent to a foster home, but they would be supervised by Social Services in the home. Only extreme cases would be removed from the family."

"It sounds promising, but what do I know," said Wanda.

"The objective of the new regulations is to reunite families and make sure they have lasting connections with their siblings."

"I don't think most of the parents are worth the time. If they were concerned about their children they would have tried to better their situation."

"Wanda, looking through the records I see you have a large number of adoption placements."

"Thank the judge and Ira. Most of the children I receive eventually are adopted. What a blessing for them to go to good and loving families."

"Who are the attorneys representing the adoptive parents?"

"It varies," said Wanda.

Suddenly she became very defensive and terminated the conversation. Rameriz thanked her for her time and scheduled another appointment for the next month.

CHAPTER 61

———◆———

JOHN WAS WAITING FOR HIS CASE to be called, sitting in the attorney lounge reading his notes. Ira entered.

"Have you seen Rameriz?"

"No."

"If you do, have him call me. I need to meet with him."

"Ira, is there any chance of avoiding adoption in the Jones case?"

"No. It's over with John; get on with another case. The judge plans to issue a final decree at the next hearing regarding parental rights and shortly after I would expect her to accelerate the adoption."

"You're kidding. She told you this?"

"No, but I know her. She wants the Jones children gone. Stop wasting your time."

"Why wouldn't you give this young mother a break?"

"Because she's scum."

"She is ill."

"Bullshit. I have seen many Samantha Joneses in this county and they are all alike."

"Don't you have any compassion for these kids?"

"None at all. They need to stop having children and counting on the social service system to support them. They need to close their legs."

"You're disgusting," said John with a glare at Ira.

"What about the alcohol, the parties, the drugs and exposing their children to the vices."

"What drugs? Oh, you mean the false statement you tried to introduce to the court. You are a real scumbag, Ira."

The announcement blared, "Munoz -- Courtroom Three." It was John's case, and he was glad to leave.

CHAPTER 62

———◆———

NOT LONG AFTER JOHN'S CASE STARTED there was a loud commotion in the adjoining courtroom. The PA system blared,

"Code Blue, Courtroom Two."

The court officer ran for the door. John asked the sergeant,

"What happened?"

"Judge Henderson terminated the parental rights and the parents reacted to the decision."

John grabbed his cell and called Rameriz.

"I'm in Henderson's Court. She just terminated a parents' rights and the father went after the Social Services attorney."

"What was their name?"

"Munoz."

Later Rameriz called the family, but they were too upset to talk and told Rameriz to call back.

CHAPTER 63

— ◆ —

RAMERIZ DUG INTO THE COURT RECORDS and determined that the adoption of all of the foster children from Judge Henderson's court were handled by Green and Grossman Attorneys. Their offices were not in Monticello, as once thought, but in New York City. In all of the cases handled by the law firm the files were missing.

"Why?" Rameriz thought.

"There must be a connection with Sol Bernstein. How do I prove it?"

He called the judge.

"May I have a few minutes with you?"

"I'm extremely busy; hold on."

She reconsidered and gave him the time.

Colleen greeted Rameriz with,

"I don't want to talk about the Jones case."

"All right. Who is Sol Bernstein?"

"He is an attorney in New York City with very wealthy clients. Why?"

"I hear his name bandied about."

"Is that what you wanted? If so, stop wasting my time."

"What is Sol's specialty?"

"Making his clients happy."

"I can't find any of your case files regarding the adoptions."

"Have you called the Records Department?"

"Yes; they're missing."

"Well then, you're shit out of luck."

Rameriz stormed out of the judge's office.

CHAPTER 64

———◆———

S AMANTHA BELIEVED HER CHILDREN were stolen by the court. As she pondered the outcome of what would happen to her little girls if they were removed and adopted, her depression was getting worse. She exhibited minimal energy and was sleeping excessively. To make matters worse, she was mixing antidepressants and alcohol and experiencing side effects ... hallucinations and thoughts of suicide.

As Samantha turned her focus to the upcoming adoption hearing, she still clung to the hope that the judge would reverse her decision, but realized it was unlikely. She started to cry.

If the decision were to take away her children and continue foster care placement, at least she might receive visitation. But if they terminated her parental rights and proceeded with adoption, her children would be gone forever.

CHAPTER 65

H ER FAVORITE BAR WAS THE "PURPLE ONION."
The stress was taking a toll on Samantha. The night before the hearing on the removal of her parental rights, she went there. She was surprised to see it was empty and asked Kattie, the barmaid,

"Where did they all go?"

"I don't know. I guess it's just a slow night."

After sipping beer for an hour and watching TV, the front door of the bar opened and a chunky, dirty looking dude staggered in.

"How ya doing, Samantha?"

"Is that you, George? I thought you were serving time."

"Just got out."

"How have you been?"

"I'm ok."

"Sit down, George. I'll buy you a beer."

"Okay."

He was glad to have conversation and listened as Samantha spent the next hour explaining her problem.

"Man, that's low."

"I know. It feels better to tell somebody about it. Where are you staying tonight?"

"I don't know."

"Do you want to flop at my house?"

"Cool."

As the two staggered towards the apartment house they barely made it up the front stairs. As they fell against the door, it opened and they both slumped to the floor.

"George, you sleep in the bedroom."

"Where's the bed?"

"Sleep on the mattress."

"How about a beer?"

"Help yourself."

"I don't want to drink alone; come on, Sam. Drink with me."

As they continued to finish one can after another, their speech slurred and they could barely keep their eyes open.

"How about a joint, Sam?"

"Yeah."

They continued to drink and smoke pot and within a few hours, they both were unconscious.

CHAPTER 66

———◆———

SAMANTHA AWOKE FROM HER STUPOR in the morning and could barely function.

"What time is it?"

"Eight thirty," said George.

"I have to be in court at nine. Holy shit! Where are my pants?" she screamed out.

"I don't know."

Samantha grabbed a top, found another pair of jeans, stuck her feet into flip flops and headed out the door. When she reached her truck, tremors made her hands so unsteady she could not start it. After a few minutes of effort and maneuvering to the tune of creative curse words, it started.

Fifteen minutes later she pulled into the Family Court parking lot. Samantha slammed the truck into park, ran through the double doors and down the hallway.

CHAPTER 67

⟞◆⟝

THE COURT OFFICER GLANCED AT SAMANTHA in recognition and advised,

"Jones ... they just called your case ... Courtroom Two."

"Thanks."

As Samantha walked into the courtroom all eyes were on her. Her clothing was severely wrinkled, her jeans had holes in the rear exposing her panties and her hair was not combed.

John pulled her over to him,

"I thought you were going to dress appropriately. I told you we had to make a good impression. Is this what you call a good impression?"

Samantha did not bother to reply and defiantly sat down. Observing the Social Services group staring, she yelled at them,

"What are you looking at?"

John tugged on her top and sternly whispered,

"Shut up!"

Samantha continued to look around the courtroom and did not see Rameriz.

"Hmmm. I wonder where he is."

"Court is in session. Judge Colleen Henderson presiding. All rise."

"Call the roll," Judge Henderson instructed in her usual tert perfunctory manner.

"Anna Frank, Social Services;

"Ira Tietz – Attorney, Social Services;

"Roberta Black – Guardian ad litem and attorney for the children;

"Samantha Jones;

"John Rainer -- Attorney for Miss Jones."

"Mr. Tietz, does the agency have any more to add to the record?"

"No, Your Honor."

"Ms. Black?"

"Nothing, Your Honor."

"Mr. Rainer?"

"I would like to make a closing statement."

"Make it short, Mr. Rainer."

CHAPTER 68

———◆———

JOHN REMINDED THE COURT of Samantha's background and all she had endured.

"Miss Jones' depression could be the main cause of her behavior. Because of an erratic policy on medication there have been many peaks and valleys. Social Services has been inconsistent in providing Miss Jones' treatment.

"Social Services would rather get the paperwork done then address a critical medical issue for my client.

"We have submitted to the court an alternative plan for the well-being of the children which would include temporary incarceration for their mother's treatment of her depression and alcohol.

"The children would remain in foster care until Miss Jones has shown progress. All visitation would be supervised, thus removing any unforeseen but possible perceived risks to these precious little twins, while they continued to receive the love and attention of their mother."

"Are you finished Mr. Rainer?"

"Yes, Your Honor."

"Miss Jones, I see you did not get the message on dress code."

John turned to Samantha with a reprimanding, I-told-you-so look.

"Miss Jones, is there anything you want to tell the court before I enter a final decree?"

CHAPTER 69

——◆——

S AMANTHA ROSE FROM HER SEAT and said: "I have made
many mistakes in my life and I truly regret my actions. If
you can see it in your heart, I will do everything possible to be
sure that I provide my children with the best possible home.
I am willing to agree to incarceration for my depression and
alcohol, and agree to no visitation with my children until
progress has been made. Please don't take away my parental
rights. I love my children. Please don't."

Judge Hendersen steadiy gazed at Samantha with a
deadpan expression that could have bored a hole in the floor
and asked in a flat voice devoid of emotion or even tenor,

"Miss Jones, are you through with your statement?"

"Yes."

"I have reviewed the evidence in the case and I have
many concerns about returning the children to your custody.

"Your irresponsible behavior in not dealing with your
depression and alcohol problem gives me great doubt about
your ability to provide the children with a good home.

"I must conclude that from the facts presented and your behavior; you are unfit."

There was a collective deep sigh in the courtroom as the judge continued.

"Therefore, I hereby decree that Jodi and Angel Jones shall be removed from your custody and your parental rights be terminated."

John held Samantha's hand and waited for the judge to rule on a hearing for adoption.

"Because you have proven to this court you have *no redemptive qualities*, I am waiving the time constraint for placing the children up for adoption.

"I am directing Social Services to proceed with the placement of the children."

As the judge finished her statement there was dead silence … time stopped … the inveterate pin did not drop.

"NO! You can't have my children!!!" Samantha screamed.

John Rainer jumped up from his seat,

"Your Honor, I respectfully ask you to rethink your decision."

"Sit down, Mr. Rainer! My decision is final."

"Your Honor, this is illegal. You have no right to do this."

"Mr. Rainer, you are bordering on contempt."

"I will appeal," John threatened, furiously pounding on the table.

"Mr. Rainer, control yourself or I will have you removed from the courtroom."

"How can this decision be fair?"

"Mr. Rainer, I am warning you."

"You allowed Social Services to taint the court transcript with false information regarding Miss Jones' alleged drug activity."

Ira jumped up,

"I object."

John shouted even louder, "Shut up, Ira; you know you lied. Why are you doing this to her? Do you want to steal her children?"

"Mr. Rainer, you have gone too far. Remove him!"

As John was being escorted from the court, Samantha laid on the table, her back heaved, the noise of her sobs rose above the ripple of whispers and conversation throughout the court room.

CHAPTER 70

———⟫◆⟪———

DURING THE CONFUSION RAMERIZ SLIPPED into the courtroom and took a seat. No one seemed to notice him in all the confusion.

"Mr. Rameriz would you help the court officer take Miss Jones from the courtroom."

All participants were standing as Samantha was virtually dragged out. Her painful sobs could be heard, as though the walls had tears, well after she left.

There was a sound like a distant train rumble as courtroom spectators and participants talked and argued amongst themselves.

The judge ordered the court officer,

"Find Mr. Rainer and return him to the courtroom."

She pounded the gavel.

"Order in the Court! Order in the Court!"

As the courtroom settled down, the judge said to John Rainer,

"Please stand. Mr. Rainer, your conduct was outrageous. I am fining you one thousand dollars."

"Your Honor, in all my years as an attorney I have never seen such a travesty of justice as this case represents. There is something terribly wrong and I plan to get to the bottom of this illegal process."

"Mr. Rainer, I strongly suggest you keep your disrespectful comments to yourself."

"Your Honor, you can't stand the truth; that's why you are punishing me. Miss Jones is not evil; you are."

"Add another thousand dollars."

"It's a pleasure, Your Honor."

"Make that another thousand."

The judge dismissed the court, and John and Ira got into a yelling match nearing physical contact. Rameriz, back from escorting Samantha out, quickly grabbed John and pulled him away.

Outside in the hallway, Rameriz, John and the court officer tried to console Samantha. Ira walked by and started to say something.

John stopped him. "Don't say anything. You're a disgrace as an attorney and officer of the court."

Ira turned to Anna,

"See what happens when they lose."

John yelled at Ira,

"Your day is coming."

As EMTs came for the call to remove Samantha from the courthouse, John and Rameriz reached down and whispered to her,

"Their day is coming."

Chapter 71

—◆—

SUSAN DROVE UP THE WINDING ROAD leading to the hospital.

She could see the the double rotating doors and a sign on the front of a grey building, 'Harris Hospital.'

As she pulled into the turnabout, she left the car idling. A few minutes later, Samantha exited the hospital. Susan waved to her from the running car, Sam waved back and then climbed in.

As they pulled out of the hospital driveway and headed for home Susan asked,

"How are you feeling?"

"I am fine."

"Are you hungry?"

"No. I had breakfast at the hospital."

"Do you need to pick up any food from the store."

"No. I have enough at the house."

"Did they give you medicine?

"Yes, the same shit."

She was unusually quiet during the ride. Susan pulled into the driveway and Samantha slowly got out of the car. There were no goodbyes.

She very slowly walked up the stairs and into the building. As she reached the apartment, she found the front door open.

She walked in and immediately started to feel anxiety. She was having problems breathing and the walls felt like they were closing in on her. She started opening up all the windows in the apartment.

When Susan finally followed her in, her first remark was, "Holy shit, it's cold in here."

Susan did not know that Samantha had opened all of the windows. She yelled,

"I am closing the windows before I freeze my ass off. What's up with this?"

"I can't breathe."

"Where is your inhaler? Find it and use it.

"Is there anything else I can do for you, Sam?"

"No, you have done enough. Thank you, Susan."

"Did you call that Jim Ashcroft about the final decree? What does Jim do, anyway?"

"I don't know. He's a friend of Rameriz."

"You know Ramirez is a cute dude. I could go for him."

"Remember, you're married, Susan."

"Yeah, I know. But I can dream, can't I?"

CHAPTER 72

As soon as Susan left, Samantha could feel her anxiety increasing.

"I need a drink." She went to the case of beer lying on the floor.

"Oh, good; it's cold."

Several hours later Samantha had a large pile of beer cans in front of her.

"I need to get some air. What time is it? Holy shit, it's one in the morning."

As she walked up Chestnut Street she hardly noticed the darkness from the lack of street lights. She did not observe that many of the porch lights on the houses were out as well due to the time of the night.

As she reached the top of Chestnut Street she did not see a police cruiser that was parked alongside a vacant lot. As she passed it the officer called out to her,

"Are you okay?"

"Yes."

"You know it's dangerous walking the streets by yourself."

"I'm not that far away from home."

"Do you want us to follow you?"

"No, but thank you. I just need to be alone."

The cruiser pulled out and went down the street and Samantha turned around and headed for home. Upon arriving she took a beer from the case by the chair. After a few hours she tried muttering to herself, but she could hardly speak.

She rummaged through her pocket book looking for Rameriz's card. She dialed the number but only the answering machine spoke to her. Samantha left a message,

"Rameriz I am having problems; please come over."

She regretfully hung up the phone and looked for the pills the doctor had given her at the hospital. She had difficulty reading the dosage on the label and just threw back two pills, double the prescribed amount, with another beer. Between the pills and the alcohol Samantha fell into a very deep sleep.

Chapter 73

⟫◆⟪

T HE NEXT MORNING RAMERIZ LISTENED to his answering machine. After hearing Samantha's message he was worried. He dialed her number but got no answer. He jumped into his car and headed for her apartment on Academy.

As he reached her apartment he noticed that the front door was slightly open. "Samantha … Sam …"

Silence. Too quiet.

As he walked into the apartment he noticed that all the windows in the apartment were half open.

"Samantha."

A little louder,

"SAM!!! It's freezing in here! What are you thinking?"

Rameriz went into the children's room and found Samantha unresponsive and curled up in the corner clasping a small baby blanket with a satin edge.

He shook her and called her name several times. Nothing. He filled the tub and placed her into the cold water. He continued to look for signs of life. There were none.

He thought he felt a pulse and decided to call for emergency assistance then heard a faint groaning.

Rameriz quickly tried to make Samantha talk but she kept groaning. Then she started talking to her children:

"Don't go out without your coat, Jodi.

"Make sure to hold hands when you are walking.

"Don't cross the street, Angel."

Then Samantha started screaming,

"I love you!"

Rameriz suspected she could be hallucinating from the beer and pills. Just as he started to dial the emergency operator, Samantha asked,

"Where am I?"

"In your apartment. You may have overdosed."

No response.

He removed her wet clothes and put a blanket around her. He removed her pants, grabbed a towel and wiped her still-silky blond hair, young curvaceous body and long legs and dressed her with a dry pair of pants, a top and a sweat shirt. She seemed to respond to his care.

Samantha opened her eyes and started to talk, repeated what happened in court, then broke down and started wailing.

Rameriz lifted her off the floor and onto the couch. After a few minutes Samantha feebly confided,

"If I don't have my children I can't go on. I might just as well kill myself."

Rameriz was startled by Samantha's remarks. He knew that her rights were taken away and the adoption was set for acceleration. The decision did not make any sense.

"Why were they acting that way?"

CHAPTER 74

———◆———

RAMERIZ CANCELLED THE EMERGENCY request and stayed with Samantha while she recovered. Later in the morning he suggested they call Tom Ashcroft.

"Hey Tom, this is Rameriz. I am here with Samantha Jones. The judge made a final decision to terminiate her parental rights and is planning to expedite the adoption, but with no hearing on the acceleration."

"Now that's unusual. Can you get me the case file?"

"I'll try. But they are already suspicious. Maybe John can help. I'll call him."

Rameriz immediately phoned John. "I need a favor. Can you get me the case file on Samantha Jones?"

"Yes, but it may take a few days.

"Send it to Tom Ashcroft in Albany, please."

Chapter 75

—◈—

Rameriz turned to Samantha on another subject. "You have a problem. You are an alcoholic. Some time ago I had the same problem and I am in AA today. If you want to have any chance of getting your kids back, you need to straighten out your drinking."

"I don't have a problem; it's that I get upset when things go upside down."

"My acquaintance is a counsellor; I am going to ask him to watch over you while I go to family court. I'm not saying anything to him; that is your choice."

"What is his name?"

"Bill Jenkins."

"Who does he work for?"

"Saint Peter's Roman Catholic Church. He could even know you. I'll call him now."

Rameriz was able to get right through.

"Hello, Bill. I have a young woman who has a problem. I need someone to watch over her while I am in court. Can you do that for me?"

"Sure; where does she live?"

"122 Academy Street."

"I'll be there in ten minutes."

Rameriz turned to Samantha,

"Don't give this guy a hard time. Understand me?"

She nodded her head and drifted back to sleep.

Later that morning when she heard conversation, Samantha came out of her bedroom,

"Who are you?"

"A friend from AA."

"I don't need a babysitter."

Rameriz held up his hand for her to stop, "Bill is not a babysitter; he is here to help you if you want it. I have to go to family court."

"Okay," Samantha said, acquiescing.

Chapter 76

——◆——

IRA WALKED INTO JUDGE HENDERSON'S OFFICE at 9:00 a.m.

"Good morning, Judge."

"Good morning, Ira."

"Have you heard any scuttlebutt about the investigation?"

"I heard from a friend in Albany that it is a special investigation and it is about adoptions for money."

"What counties are included?"

"Orange, Sullivan and Dutchess."

"Who is working on the investigative team?"

"The best that I can determine is the State Police and special investigators from the Attorney General's Office. All the details are being held in total secrecy. This is not good for us, Colleen. Something could point in our direction. I don't like it. "

"Relax. What do you think I sealed all the records for, Ira. I hope you're not getting cold feet. Isn't all that money you've made enough to offset some misplaced insecurity? I've got a lot on my mind. Don't add to it. Don't make me worry about you. Do you think Rameriz could be involved?"

"Are you kidding? Look at him. He is a nerd, a math wizard. He is no investigator."

"Tell your folks to keep us informed; let us know if they get any clues."

"Okay."

"How are we doing on the Jones file?" asked Colleen.

"I have all the paperwork done; do you want to have another hearing?"

"Absolutely not. I don't want to give John another bite of the apple. Just ram it through, Ira. What are we doing to cover ourselves about Samantha's background?"

"What do you want to do?"

"I want you to get to the Liberty Police undercover agent and have him prepare a fake affidavit about the drugs. We need to firm up our case in the event it's reviewed by Albany. I want you to stop fucking around and get this adoption closed."

"Okay, Colleen."

"By the way, have you spoken to Wanda?"

"No."

"I want that taken care of today and I don't want any loose ends. Let's meet later and discuss what she had to say."

CHAPTER 77

IRA LEFT THE JUDGE'S CHAMBERS and promptly called Wanda.

"I need to see you today."

"What is my cut?"

"I thought you were going to talk to the judge?"

"I did; that bitch did not want to part with anything."

"We need to talk, Wanda. I will see you at 3:00 p.m."

"Okay."

"Marge, I'm going out on a call," Ira told his secretary.

"What is the name of the client?"

Ira ignored her and Marge just shook her head. He drove to Broadway and parked in Wanda's driveway.

She walked out to greet him.

"Why don't you come in?"

"I would rather meet outside to make sure there are no wiring devices to hear our conversation."

"You are paranoid, Ira! Are you nuts? Nobody has been tapping my phone or listening to my conversations."

"Listen, Wanda, we need to move on this issue, our parents are grumbling. When parents complain the price goes down and we lose money."

"What is my cut?"

"I'll have the judge meet with you and resolve the issue."

"That's bullshit. She does not want to part with anything. Unless she meets my demands there will be no more adoptions. I promise. Tell that bitch she better not play games with me or I will open my mouth."

"Really. Are you also planning to tell on me?" Ira asked cautiously.

"No," reassured Wanda.

"Listen. I will set up a meeting with Judge Colleen to resolve this problem once and for all."

"Okay; but it needs to be done quickly or else," threatened Wanda.

Chapter 78

———◆———

IRA MET WITH THE JUDGE LATER THAT DAY.

"So, Ira, how did it go with Wanda?"

"She wants her cut raised or she's threatening to spill the beans."

"Oh, really. That bitch has gotten over $200,000 and says she is going to report us! I hope she plans to join us in jail. "

"It's time we talk to Sol Bernstein."

"We will. Right now."

Colleen picked up the phone and dialed Sol's unlisted number.

"Sol, we have a problem. Wanda is trying to blackmail us for more money. She says if she doesn't get a bigger slice of the pie, she is going to report us to the authorities. I guess it's time for a permanent change in personnel," she said matter-of-factly.

"Do you want me to arrange the change?"

"I'll meet with her next week, and if we don't make any progress then I suggest we make a change immediately."

"Do you want me to take care of it personally?"

"Yes. Obviously, it needs to look like an accident."

"Okay; you give me the word and it will be over."

CHAPTER 79

———◆———

COLLEEN AND WANDA SCHEDULED a meeting a few days later in Goshen at the Hard Castle Restaurant. Colleen arrived first wearing a black wig and a large white hat with a wide floppy brim and sunglasses. Wanda arrived shortly afterwards looking like she just got out of a corn patch, in jeans and a John Deere green sweatshirt with a tractor on the back.

The waitress asked Colleen if she wanted lunch.

"First get me a martini."

"And you, mam?" the waitress asked Wanda.

"I'll have a Bud."

When the waitress was out of earshot, Colleen started the conversation about percentages in the adoption scheme.

"Wanda, the cost of paying off people in Albany and the undercover investigator has made the profit very marginal."

"Yeah. What cut is Sol getting? It doesn't matter he brings in the clients. So what? I make sure the clients and children hit it off. And you know that Sol is under investigation."

"I didn't know. Who told you that, Wanda?"

"Rameriz. He asked me if I knew who Sol was and if I ever met him. I said no."

"Really. Did Rameriz ask you any other questions?"

"He was curious about all my paintings and antiques. I told him I got most of the pieces from my family. If I don't get the cut that I expect then I will drop Rameriz a letter and your scam will be over."

"Is that right? And where do you think YOUR prison cell will be, Wanda? Bedford Hills?"

"All I know is I won't be alone," Wanda said with a defiant glare.

Colleen was at the height of frustration.

"You will not get a bigger cut on this job, and that is all there is to it."

Wanda stood up. "You will be sorry."

As she started to walk out she turned, "Remember I warned you."

Colleen ignored the remark and continued her lunch.

Chapter 80

---◆---

Colleen called Sol later that day.

"What's happening, Colleen?"

"Did you know that investigators are asking about you, Sol?"

"No, I didn't. Who's asking?"

"Rameriz, a special investigator who works for the Albany Court. He portrays himself as a researcher but I think it's bullshit."

"Colleen, tell Wanda that you have had second thoughts about her cut and that you will increase it as she wants."

"I am flat out not doing that."

"Okay. Let's hold her off as long as we can. Before she can blow the whistle she will be gone if you catch my drift."

"How are you going to make her be gone?

"It's better if you do not know any of the details."

"Okay," agreed Colleen.

At 5:00 p.m. Ira went to see Colleen.

"How did you make out with Wanda?" Ira asked.

"At first it was rough, but I have decided to give her what she wants"

"I don't believe it," said Ira. "Did you tell Sol?"

"Yes, he's the one who sold me on it."

"I just don't understand."

"Be patient, Ira; everything will work out. She could be gone before she even thinks of fingering us."

"Jeez, Colleen. Why does it sound like you're going to knock her off? Man, I didn't buy into that."

"Leave all of these types of details to me. I shouldn't even tell you things. I told you before I can't be worrying and babysitting you."

"Okay, okay. I got ahold of that investigator in Liberty and explained what we wanted. He will do it for 5K. I told him to go ahead and make the facts up. He said it shouldn't be very hard to frame Samantha Jones. I hope he's on the up and up and this is not his way of incriminating me, Colleen."

"No way. The police don't make that much, so 5K for him would mean something. You did great!"

"I'll see you tomorrow."

"Good night, Ira."

After Ira left Colleen dialed Wanda. She answered flatly, "What do you want?"

"I have thought about your proposal and I know you left very unhappy."

"Tell me something new."

"I have decided to give you the increase in percentage that you want."

"What's the catch?"

"No catch. I even talked to Sol who said you deserved it."

"That's great."

"Wanda, my husband is giving me a birthday party. Why don't you join us."

"Of course. Just let me know when and where."

As Colleen hung up the phone a wry smile broke out on her face.

"Now you will get what you deserve."

CHAPTER 81

———◆———

COLLEEN DROVE TO NEW YORK to attend an American Bar Association meeting, arriving at The Park Plaza Hotel on Friday morning. The doorman took her bags and she headed for the front desk.

"Judge Henderson," she announced.

"Welcome to The Park Plaza, Your Honor," said the clerk as he checked his computer then gave her the room key for 807.

"The bell hop will deliver your luggage."

"Thank you. I am expecting a guest shortly."

Within ten minutes, Sol entered the lobby. His appearance reflected that he was a distinguished, capable gentleman: 70 years old, average height, stocky and a perfectly manicured beard that hung below his chin. Sol was known as a very clever attorney with extensive underworld connections. His acquaintance with Colleen went back many years; he was the one who encouraged her to become a lawyer and then a judge. He phoned her from the lobby.

"What do you feel like doing?"

"Let's have lunch. Katz's on Houston Street has an excellent corned beef sandwich."

"Okay. I know the place."

Colleen came down and Sol hailed a cab and directed the driver to the deli.

After finishing lunch, they left Katz's and started walking towards the train station. As they were crossing the avenue a black BMW with New Jersey plates came speeding up. At first Sol and Colleen just stayed in the crosswalk. However, as the car got closer it seemed to be heading for them. Sol said to Colleen,

"Get back on the sidewalk."

They hurried, but the faster they ran to avoid the car, the more it accelerated, directly towards them. The car swerved and just missed them, made a sharp right, disappeared and went down the next block. It stopped and idled, as if the person inside were watching them.

Sol said unconvincingly, "It's nothing."

"I don't buy that story. I think someone is trying to kill us."

"Nonsense. It's just New York."

But instead of taking the train, they hailed a cab and slouched into the back seat as they rode to The Park Plaza.

Sol pointed out the street vendor on the edge of Central Park by the horses and carriages.

"Come on, Colleen. Let's get some ice cream and sit by the golden General Sherman monument. It will take your mind off everything."

"Good idea, Sol. I love ice cream."

They asked the driver to let them out at the next signal light and got out of the taxicab. After a pleasant interlude, they waited at the crosswalk to make their way to the hotel past the fountain splashing in the pond.

Just as they stepped up onto the curb, the black BMW appeared out of nowhere, accelerating right towards Judge Henderson. She looked up in a state of panic and started running.

"Oh my God, Sol. He's back. He's trying to kill me," she screamed.

People scattered as the car bounced over the curb still on a beeline towards the judge. Sol started yelling,

"Head for the pond, Colleen. Run faster!!!"

She ran so fast she stumbled and made a mad flop, right into the pond. The black BMW casually turned and headed down Fifth Avenue, like a Sunday drive.

There was a minute of quiet; the fountain splashed.

The tourists looked aghast at the scene: Judge Colleen Henderson was sitting in the water, her clothes dripping, pushing errant strands of her hair into the bun on the back of her head, a look of disgust with traces of fear on her face.

Then there was the sound of chaos as everyone started talking at once. Sol gave Colleen a hand.

"Now don't start going apeshit on me, Colleen. Yes, it was terrible. You never know what New York drivers will do. Let me help you up. Pay no attention to everyone staring at you. We'll just get you to your room, freshen up, and you'll be fine."

Colleen did not speak but stared at Sol so hard he felt like she was boring a hole through him. He stopped talking while he surreptitiously looked around for the black BMW. They walked up the hotel steps.

The doorman indeed acted like nothing had happened and did not raise an eyebrow at Colleen dressed like a wet sewer rat.

Sol said he would wait in the lobby while she showered and changed. She still was not speaking to him.

When she came down, they were both clearly shaken by the incident and decided to have a night cap to calm their nerves. Sol refused to belabor a discussion of the incident.

"It's just a New York event. On a more important subject, Colleen, the prospective adoptive parents are complaining that the process is taking too long."

"I assure you I am moving as fast as possible to have the children become eligible for adoption, Sol.

"Fine. Tell me about the inquiry by the State Police and their investigation of you."

"Look; I told you that there was nothing to the story. Let's drop it."

As Colleen was leaving to attend her ABA meeting she stopped for messages. The desk clerk handed her an envelope. She opened it.

"We know what you doing and we are going to punish you all."

"Who left this message?" Colleen immediately asked the front desk clerk.

"A young boy said he was told to deliver it to Judge Henderson, Room 807."

Colleen immediately called Sol. "We have a problem."

"What is it?"

"Someone left a note for me at the front desk," and she read it to him.

"What should we do, Sol?"

"Maybe it's Wanda?"

"No. She is satisfied for now with the increased cut. We need to discuss Ira, too; he's becoming a wus about the police, Wanda, your investigation, and the beat goes on. But Sol, you are taking care of our problem with Wanda?"

"Yes, it's being worked on."

"Okay."

"Don't forget that after our ABA meeting we are having dinner with some new clients tonight. I will pick you up at 7 p.m."

"Where are we eating?"

"Del Posta in Chelsea."

There was a sense of normalcy as the evening wore on. After a wonderful meal and a very successful meeting with prospective parents Colleen was feeling good; she thanked Sol for his support.

On the way back from the restaurant Colleen announced, "I want the charge to be $70,000 per child."

Sol disagreed, "They already went up to $100 to $125k for the two of them. Your price is too high."

"These are beautiful children -- blonde hair, blue eyes; what could be better."

"The price is too high. My client will go up to a max of the $125,000 for both of the twin girls."

"No. This was a tough case and still is, so we need to get paid more for our services. That's only right."

"Colleen, you are getting greedy, but I'll see what I can do. Let's talk in the morning."

The next morning the judge was still stewing about the BMW and called Sol.

"Do you think I should call the police?"

"No. Let's kept them out of our business."

"Okay. I will call you when I get back to Sullivan County. I want you to confirm the purchase price of the children. I won't take any less than 70k apiece. After all the cuts come out, that's fair."

"It will be a tough sell."

Chapter 82

—◆—

RAMERIZ CALLED SAMANTHA.

"How are you feeling?"

"I can't get over the loss of the kids."

"I know how you must feel, Sam; try to remember that this case is not over. I know it looks bad, but we still can find a solution to our problem."

Samantha snickered,

"That's all I have kept hearing since the case started … it will get better. I've lost my parental rights and my children while waiting for it to get better. I don't have much faith in the system."

"I understand," Rameriz said with compassion.

"Goodbye, Rameriz."

She hung up the phone, sat down on the couch with her face in her hands and started to cry.

"What have I done? I can't believe I can't find anyone who will help me."

Later that night Samantha took her medication and started drinking. She was well aware of the dangers of this behavior, but she was having problems dealing with the loss. By midnight, she still couldn't sleep and her anxiety was hitting a peak. She popped another anti-depression pill and washed it down with beer, staggered over to the couch and fell asleep.

Rameriz called Samantha about 1:00 a.m. Samantha was groggy as she answered.

"You don't sound right, Sam. Are you okay?"

"I took my pills … I'm not sure how many. I was drinking. I can't seem to focus."

"Go back to sleep. I'll see you in the morning."

"Okay," she said, and swallowed three more pills then soon fell into an unconscious state.

Rameriz called Samantha in the morning. No answer. He left a message,

"I would like to meet with you and go over the case."

When Samantha woke up, she could barely function. She saw the light on the phone blinking and listened to the message.

"What's the use; I've lost my babies already."

She went back to bed and Rameriz called again.

"Samantha, please do as I ask; maybe we can help you."

Hearing Rameriz's voice, she staggered to the phone and answered.

"Where do you want me to meet you?" he asked.

"Let's meet at John's office. I am sure he won't mind. What time?"

"10 o'clock."

"Okay."

CHAPTER 83

———◆———

SAMANTHA DROVE TO JOHN'S OFFICE. As she entered she caught a glimpse of John and Rameriz in the conference room and walked in. John gave Samantha a hug,

"We are still in the game. I have to go out. You and Rameriz are welcome to stay here as long as you wish."

She just nodded. Rameriz motioned for her to sit down and asked,

"Have you gotten your medical insurance?"

"No. There is some problem with the paperwork."

Rameriz slammed his fist on the table.

"What the hell is going on? You should have had it by now. I am going to see Ira and talk to him.

"Samantha, is it true you were homeless?"

"No, I had an apartment."

"Is it true you got food from the food bank?"

"Yes, I would go there. So did other people."

"When you had the party were the children present?"

"No, they were at Susan's house."

"Let's talk about Social Services. Did they help you?"

"Sometimes, but they did not help me get any medication. I have the benefits, then I lose them, and I never know why."

"Let's talk about your drinking? Have you started dealing with your problem like I suggested?"

"Yes. And I told the court I was willing to go into rehab or do whatever they suggested."

"Finally, what about the condition of the house?"

"I agree it was a mess. Anna from Social Services was probably right about removing the children, but to take them away from me forever ... I don't see why ...."

Rameriz was very serious throughout the interview.

"What they never talk about is how much my depression affected me, and also that I could not get the medicine I need that helps."

"What about the drugs, Sam?"

"It's true I have smoked weed, but nothing harder. I swear on my children's souls, the story they told in court was a lie. And as for the prostitution charge it was nothing. I got an appearance ticket for loitering and eventually the thing was just dismissed."

They walked to her car and said goodbyes laced with commiseration.

CHAPTER 84

RAMERIZ CALLED JOHN.

"I finished speaking with Samantha and I asked her all the sensitive questions regarding the case. I don't understand why the judge was so harsh."

"I agree, but there is something else going on. The judge and Social Services seem to be protecting the children from the mother, but for what reason. I have a feeling that Ira is behind this whole process."

"What about the judge?"

"I doubt it, but you can never tell."

"How would they get the children if a judge was not involved?"

"I don't know."

Rameriz decided to call the chief judge and determine if there was merit to the case. He got through and was able to set an appointment to meet with Judge Hyde.

As he walked down the hallway, he heard a legal assistant talking to someone named Ira. At first Rameriz paid no attention, but then he heard the legal assistant mention Judge Henderson.

"Was this Ira's mole in Albany?" he concluded.

The chief judge's secretary called Rameriz.

"He is waiting for you."

Rameriz entered the office.

"Good morning, Your Honor. How are you?"

"How's it going?"

"Okay. I think I have a lead on the people involved in the adoption scheme. We are getting closer."

"What can I do for you?"

"There is a case in Sullivan County; her name is Samantha Jones. It involves her twin little girls. The judge appears to have completely ignored the facts and is rushing the decision on terminating parental rights and placing the children up for adoption. I am not getting any straight answers."

"So what do you want?"

"I want you to review the file."

"Rameriz, I can't overrule another judge unless there is blatant unethical behavior."

"Could you just review the transcript? Please."

"Rameriz, don't take any chances; these could be dangerous people."

"I will be careful, but I have to try to help this person; she is getting a raw deal. What is worse is that I have a feeling this is part of the adoption ring. The blond, blue-eyed physical attributes of children fit the profile."

"Anything else?"

Yes, the legal assistant that works for you; is she new?"

"Yes. Why do you ask?"

"Just inquiring."

Later in the day Rameriz called Ira and Colleen and made an appointment to see them the next day.

The next morning Rameriz went to Ira's office.

"Good morning, Ira."

Ira kept looking down and failed to acknowledge Rameriz. He took a seat and waited for Ira to speak.

"What's up?" said Ira after the thinly disguised delay for a heavy workload.

"I guess I owe you an apology about our last meeting. Did you check me out?"

"Yes, and you are who you say you are."

"I am relieved I am me," said Rameriz with a touch of witty sarcasm.

"During your meeting with Wanda, why were you so interested in Sol and why bring him up to her?"

"I heard his name mentioned and I know he deals with adoptions. Wanda did not know him. Do you know him?"

"I know he is a friend of Judge Henderson."

"Tell me, Ira, why does Samantha Jones not have her medical benefits?"

"Why are you asking me? Let's ask her social worker."

"What do you think about the new adoption rules and regulations?"

Ira responded quickly, "I support a better system."

Rameriz sensed Ira was brushing him off.

"Tell me about your contacts in Albany."

"The only person I know is a woman who works in the

chief judge's office as a legal secretary. She has been there for years."

"Oh, I thought she was new. I guess I got it wrong," said Rameriz.

CHAPTER 85

⤙◆⤚

RAMERIZ MET WITH COLLEEN HENDERSON.
"Good Afternoon, Judge."

Judge Henderson remained silent.

"Have you read the proposal for the new adoptions policy?"

"Yes."

"What do you think of it?"

"I think it stinks."

"Why?"

"We don't have the manpower. Who is going to pay for the additional cost? The state? You have got to be kidding."

"What's up with Samantha Jones?"

"Why do you ask?"

"Just curious."

"It's none of your business, so don't ask."

Judge Henderson changed the subject and put on a phony smile.

"My husband is giving me a birthday party. Why don't you join us?"

"Sure, that would be great."

"I'll let you know the date and time."

CHAPTER 86

———◆———

SAMANTHA SAT ON THE COUCH THINKING about her little girls. Suddenly she decided to call her friend.

"Susan, it's Sam. What do you think about this idea?"

"What idea?"

"I will tell you; just hold your water. I was thinking of calling Peter."

"The children's father? You're kidding."

"I will tell him what is happening and ask him to get involved. Maybe he could get custody."

"Are you crazy? The Peter who has not called you since the twins were born? The Peter who wanted the children killed before they were even born?"

"Yes. I mean let's call him."

"You have got to be kidding. I would not let him take care of my dog."

After thinking about Susan's comments, Samantha agreed and hung up the phone.

CHAPTER 87

———◆———

RAMERIZ CALLED SAMANTHA.
"How are you doing?"

"Not good. I was talking to Susan about the girls."

"Sam, you have to try and focus on getting them back."

"I am. What do you think I'm doing?

"Rameriz, what do you do for a living? You have been very vague."

"Let's say I am working on a new proposal to reunite children with their parents."

"How do you feel about adoptions?"

"I want to limit adoptions to the worst situations."

"Do you work for the court?"

"Well, sort of."

"Then you can help me."

"Yes and no."

"Would you consider adopting the twins?"

"I can't. How is your depression?"

"I think it's getting worse."

"How about the medicine?"

"I take it when I get it from the hospital. But nothing is working."

CHAPTER 88

—◆—

"I HAVE BAD NEWS, RAMERIZ," was John's opening when he phoned the undercover investigator.

"What is it?"

"The judge has entered an order to accelerate the adoption of the Jones children. It's over."

"Did you tell Sam?"

"No. I would rather tell her in person."

"Wait till morning, John."

"Okay."

The next morning John called Samantha.

"Do you think you can find a way to my office?"

"Sure. What do you need?"

"I'll tell you when you get here."

"I'll see you at 9:30."

Samantha drove to John's office with some expectation that the news would be good. As she pulled into the parking lot John was sitting on the bench outside his office. This was surely out of character for him.

"What's up?"

"Sit down. Sam, I have bad news. The judge has approved the acceleration of the children's adoption. A family has been selected and the process has started."

"But this case just happened ..."

John was silent then started to talk, but Samantha held up her hand to him. John started again, but she interrupted,

"Don't. No more."

She then got up and headed for her truck. John stood there silent until she drove off, then turned and purposefuly strode back into his office. He called Rameriz.

"What's up?" asked Rameriz.

"I just informed Sam that the adoption of the twins was approved."

"Oh my God. She must be heartbroken."

CHAPTER 89

—◆—

S AMANTHA ENTERED HER APARTMENT. She looked into
the babies' room. She went into the kitchen and grabbed a
beer. After an hour one beer became many beers.

Rameriz called; she didn't answer; he left a message:
"Please call me."

Samantha refused to pick up the phone. For hours she
sat in her chair and stared at the ceiling.

At 12:00 a.m. Sam called Rameriz's house and left a message:
"I love you. Thanks for everything."

Rameriz was on duty at work, thinking about Samantha
and getting concerned because she had not called him back
on his business phone.

By 2:00 a.m. Samantha started taking her meds; one at a
time, then she swallowed the whole bottle.

By 3:00 a.m. she was unconscious and lying on the floor
of the apartment.

As Rameriz got off duty he headed for Samantha's apartment. He knocked on the door. No answer. He started banging on the door. Nothing. Finally, he kicked the apartment door down, cracking the frame, entered and yelled,

"Samantha, where are you?"

Silence.

He checked each room and closet, then spotted Samantha's body on the floor. Rameriz grabbed her wrist and checked for a pulse. No response. He took it again. No response. He dialed the operator and reported an emergency, told the operator the location and the fact that he could not get a pulse.

Rameriz picked up Samantha and carried her to the shower. As he looked into her face his sense of concern grew. The cool water stirred no response. In desperation he slapped her face and applied CPR, but still no response. He was losing all hope and cried out,

"Why? What did she ever do?"

Suddenly the paramedics blustered into the apartment and Rameriz yelled out,

"In here."

As the paramedics began working on Samantha, Rameriz pushed back from her limp body and sat on the floor. They tried to find life. They looked at Rameriz and shook their heads.

"This young lady is dead."

He felt wooden.

The police arrived and Rameriz explained what he knew about Samantha's death. Shortly afterwards the Medical Examiner arrived, pronounced her legally dead and began collecting evidence. The body was removed for autopsy at Harris Hospital.

Rameriz called John. "I have bad news."

"Yes ...."

"Samantha is dead ...."

John could hardly speak but finally mumbled something then yelled out,

"Nooooo....." and started to cry.

"How?" he squeaked out, his voice breaking as though the simple word had more than one syllable.

"It looks like drugs, but we're not sure. Samantha just couldn't take any more. The children were the last straw."

John sobbed,

"Their day is coming," and hung up.

CHAPTER 90

---◆---

A S THE FAMILY GATHERED outside the funeral home waiting to enter, Rose and Henry barely spoke. They were feeling the strain of losing their youngest daughter and the guilt of not being supportive since they made her leave home.

Joining Rose and Henry were her sisters, aunts, uncles, Rameriz and Susan. Samantha would have been impressed with the number of people in attendance.

The one person unbeknown to most was a good looking young man with blue eyes and blond hair. He acted like he wanted to go unnoticed.

Most notable was the absence of John Rainer, the attorney who had become the friend and valiant knight of the tragic young mother.

As they prepared to enter the funeral home they all engaged in small talk. The funeral parlor door opened and the crowd entered the viewing room.

The first to see Samantha in her casket was Henry. He could not stop the tears from flowing; Rose tried to console him but had differculty holding herself together. After a few minutes, Henry and Rose took their seat in the front row.

As the visitors passed the coffin and paid their final respects, all of the family seemed numbed by the event.

When Rameriz paid his respects he noted how well dressed Samantha was and her hair was styled. He sadly thought to himself,

"What a beautiful girl."

Towards the later part of the services the young man with golden blond hair and blue eyes entered the viewing room. He went to the coffin and after a few minutes you could see him wiping the tears from his eyes. He did not stop and pay his respects to the family but instead headed for the back of the room. As he sat there alone he was immediately confronted by Susan.

"You have some nerve coming to her funeral. You are nothing but a low life."

As Susan got louder and louder Peter quietly got up to leave. She followed him out the door yelling at him that he abandoned Samantha and the twins.

Peter was taken aback to learn that Samantha (and he) had twins. He started to ask Susan a question when Rameriz came out to see what the commotion was all about. Susan said to Rameriz that Peter was a low life but never explained who he was, not wanting to validate any involvement with Samantha, much less that he was the father of her little girls.

As the funeral services concluded, all of the family left and went to Rose and Henry's house.

CHAPTER 91

---◆---

JOHN WAS FEELING THE EFFECTS of Samantha's death and his inability to win the case. In an effort to keep the children with her parents he decided to call Rose and Henry and meet with them. His goal was to convince them to consider the adoption of the twins. He picked up the phone. Rose answered.

"Hello, this is John Rainer, and I was Samantha's attorney. Please accept my condolences. I would like to meet with you and your husband tonight."

"Let me talk to Henry and I will call you back."

Rose picked up the phone and called Henry at work.

"John Rainer, Samantha's attorney wants to meet with us."

"What does he want?"

"He didn't say."

"I hope he's not looking for money."

"I doubt it," Rose said, a sound of disgust in her voice.

After a long pause,

"Okay."

Rose called John back and they confirmed the time and their home address.

At 7 p.m. John pulled his dark grey, almost black, BMW into the front yard. Rose was already standing on the porch stairs. As he got out of his car, he greeted her then followed her into the house.

As he entered, an air of familiarity overcame him … like he'd been there before. A large, robust man was sitting in his recliner and nodded as John came through the door. He took a seat on the couch.

"I am very sorry for your loss, Mr. and Mrs. Jones."

Neither Henry nor Rose responded.

"As you know, the court approved the adoption."

"Why are you telling us?" Henry inquired.

"I would like to propose a plan in order to get the children returned to you."

Rose looked at Henry, but both were silent.

John asked,

"Are you interested in getting custody?"

Rose looked at Henry's face and it was expressionless. She said nervously,

"Of course."

Henry raised his hand as if to stop his wife from speaking, then said,

"We can't."

"These are your granddaughters."

"We just can't."

Rose stared at the floor and was silent.

Henry said to John,

"We'd love to, but it's not possible."

John's face reflected his frustration and he felt sure that they had no interest in the children, any more than they had when Samantha struggled all alone, any more than they had when she fought in court, barely more than a child herself. He reluctantly gave up, hoping the adoptive parents would give the twins more love and support than Samantha had gotten.

After their decision, he exchanged small talk with them and answered the perfunctory questions about his background.

"I grew up on the west coast but was born in Livingston Manor. I was adopted."

Rose asked,

"Did you know your birth mother?"

John surprised Rose and Henry with,

"Yes. But she passed away."

"Sorry to hear that. What was her name?"

John gave her name absentmindly, "Mary Roser," and added, "She lived on Candlestick Road."

Henry was silent and studied John's face with great intensity. Rose also stared at him. The visit and conversation concluded and he left.

Henry and Rose stared at each other. Then she said,

"John Rainer is your son."

Henry could hardly speak. John Rainer was Samantha's brother. John Rainer was the child he had given up for adoption. Deja vu.

"I can't believe it."

He got up from his chair and went upstairs to his room.

CHAPTER 92

—◆—

RAMERIZ CONTACTED JOHN the next day.
"How come I did not see you at the funeral? I could not believe you missed it."

"I just couldn't handle seeing Samantha because I feel so responsible for her death. I failed her."

"You're not responsible. You did the best you could for her."

John let the reassurance pass.

"Has the medical examiner determined the cause of death?"

"No. It's probably an overdose of drugs and alcohol. I've got to believe the news of losing the children to adoption, never to see them again, pushed her over the edge."

"You're probably right, but we will never know will we, Rameriz?"

"I am meeting with Ira to see if the adoption records are available for review. The last time I inquired about the information I got nowhere. They stonewalled my request."

Chapter 93

———◆———

Rameriz entered Ira's office.

"Sorry about Samantha," said Ira.

Rameriz stared at Ira knowing how meaningless the statement was and refused to respond.

"Ira, in the interest of my work on foster care and adoption, I would like to review the case files on Jones."

"Why that case?"

"It fits my research criteria."

"How about choosing another case?"

"I really want *that* case."

"Well, if I remember correctly, those case files were sealed by Judge Henderson."

"Why?"

"You'll have to ask her."

"Does she seal all adoption case files?"

"No, just some."

"Do you think she will unseal the file?"

"I doubt it, but you could ask. When do you plan to complete your research?"

"Why? Do you want to get rid of me?" Rameriz said with a sardonic smile.

"No; just inquiring."

"Do you think Judge Henderson is available?"

"Let me call and see if she has time for you."

"Colleen, I am with Rameriz. He would like to meet with you about unsealing the Jones adoption files. Do you have time? I will tell him that."

As Ira hung up the phone he advised Rameriz,

"She will not unseal the Jones file. She is very busy."

Rameriz thanked Ira and left.

CHAPTER 94

—◆—

JOHN CALLED IRA later on in the day.

"Can you do me a favor."

"What is it?"

"Were the Jones children in any other foster homes than Wanda's prior to adoption?"

"Why do you ask?"

"I need the addresses for my files and the name of the foster care mothers."

"No, it was just Wanda. If you don't have it already, the foster home is located at 8 Hillcrest Road in Monticello."

"Thanks for the information. Now my files are complete."

CHAPTER 95

---◆---

R AMERIZ CONTACTED JUDGE HYDE in Albany later that day.

"Your Honor, I regret to report that Samantha Jones, the young mother of the twins, has committed suicide."

"I am sorry," said the judge.

"I know how you felt about her and the way they treated her. We still have a job to get done."

"I know."

Rameriz started investigating the foster home owners. He ran a credit check and reviewed the tax returns filed with the IRS.

Wanda and Bill had substantial assets as he had seen when he was in their home, not inherited as Wanda had claimed, but rather they had a series of purchases of expensive art. The tax returns showed moderate income that did not match up with the assets they had accumulated.

Rameriz called Wanda. "I would like to set up a meeting with you and Bill tomorrow."

"What about?"

"The role of foster care and salaries for the personnel who supervise the children."

Rameriz baited Wanda by telling her how well off Judge Henderson was and how she just recently bought a new Corvette convertible.

Wanda started to tell Rameriz something then stopped,

"All I can tell you is that she will need....."

"What do you mean?"

"I'll see you tomorrow," replied Wanda and terminated the call.

CHAPTER 96

—◆—

WANDA CALLED IRA AT HOME. "I want to meet with you somewhere away from Liberty."

"Where?"

"How about the restaurant in Callicoon -- The Hay Seed."

"Okay. What time?"

"2:30."

Wanda walked into the restaurant and started looking for Ira. She found him sitting at a table in the rear staring out the window. She waved and joined him.

"How are you?"

"Sit down."

Wanda took a sip of water and placed the glass down on the table.

"Do you want more water?"

"No, Ira. When is the judge going to give me my cut?"

"You have to be patient. The adoption is not complete."

"Bullshit! I want my money. If I don't get my money soon you're all going to jail."

"Wanda, you can't keep threatening the judge. You're pushing her to the limit."

"What is she going to do, send Sol after me? He will go down with the rest of us."

Ira became frustrated with the conversation and finally said,

"Enough. I will get back to you. You're impossible. You have made a substantial amount of money with us. Have some faith."

Wanda finally agreed and they finished their lunch with meaningless conversation.

CHAPTER 97

———◆———

R AMERIZ VISTIED WANDA AT HER HOME.
"Thank you for seeing me."

She nodded.

"Wanda, I represent an agency in Albany studying foster care and adoption as I have previously told you. I would like to go over how your operation works and discuss your ideas on adoption. Is your husband here?"

"No. I will answer all your questions."

"I would like to talk to you both."

"Our meeting then will have to be another day."

"How about Wednesday at 9:30 in the morning?"

"Great."

Rameriz left Wanda's house with a great deal of suspicion about why her husband was not available. He called Tom Ashcroft and briefed him on his meeting and the rescheduling because Wanda's husband was not available.

"Rameriz, do not get too aggressive … we don't want to spook them … they are dangerous. By the way, what's the word on the attorney named Sol? We are trying to build a case against him for money laundering. But we haven't been able to connect him to adoptions for money."

"We have to get someone to roll over and give us the evidence we need for a conviction, Tom. I'll keep working on it."

On Wednesday Rameriz went back to see Wanda. He rang the doorbell and Wanda answered,

"Please come in."

As Rameriz entered the house he was again taken back by the amount of expensive artwork and furniture. He knew she could not afford all these antiques and paintings on her salary. While he was admiring her artwork he noticed two little girls in an adjoining bedroom. He thought they must be the Jones twins.

As soon as Wanda saw Rameriz watching the girls she closed the door.

"So tell me, what do you want to know?"

"The last time I was here we rescheduled so I could speak with both you and your husband. Is he joining us?

"No, Rameriz. I have the lead on this and will answer all of your questions. I told you before that Bill is on permanent disability."

"All right; let's move on then. You were not in favor of the new proposal on foster care. Do you still have the same opinion?"

"Yes. Where are they going to find all the personnel needed to supervise the children when they still live with their parents who are not fit? We don't have enough personnel now; can you imagine what a shortage will be created under this new plan."

"Can you tell me why there are so many adoptions from your court?"

"Don't talk to me; ask Ira and the judge. I do what I am told."

"I get it. What do you do for the adoptive parents?"

"I take the children to see the people interested in adopting them and report back to the judge and Ira."

"It sounds like something outside of your job description. How come the social worker doesn't handle those responsibilities?"

"You mean like Anna? That's a joke. She can't stand children."

Rameriz continued to discuss the adoption with Wanda and finally got around to Samantha's case.

"What do you think about the adoptive parents for the twins?"

"They appear to be very nice."

"Have you heard from an attorney named Sol?"

"Who is he? Haven't you asked me about him before?"

"An adoption attorney from New York City."

"Why do you ask about him?"

"He does a lot of business in Orange County and I was wondering if he had any contacts in Sullivan County."

"I don't know."

"That's all I have. Thank you for the interview, Wanda. I appreciate your time, and I hope to speak briefly with your husband one of these days."

Rameriz was sure Wanda was lying about Sol but he needed to maintain communication.

"All we need is a break," he reflected.

Wanda called Ira. "Rameriz just left. He asked questions about Sol and the Jones twins."

"What did you tell him?"

"Nothing. But if I don't get my money I will have a lot to say."

"Shut up Wanda; you'll get your cut."

CHAPTER 98

WANDA VISITED THE MEDICAL CLINIC for her yearly check-up later in the week. After a number of tests and a through examination the doctor concluded she was very healthy. No major concerns.

CHAPTER 99

————◆————

COLLEEN'S HUSBAND MADE THE PLANS to celebrate his wife Judge Henderson's 60th birthday at The Hilton Hotel in Monticello. The guest list included all of the attorneys at Family Court and their wives, court administrative personnel, friends and family.

The party was very crowded but Colleen and Sol found a small corner to talk. She whispered to Sol,

"Are you ready to deal with Wanda?"

"Yes."

As the night continued, Wanda and her husband had several drinks. Later in the evening John introduced himself.

"I am the attorney for the Jones girls."

"Yes; I heard about your behavior in the court."

"Well, there are two sides to every story."

The small talk continued and the barbed comments diminished. John offered to refresh their drinks.

"What are you drinking, Wanda?"

"Scotch and Soda."

"Does your husband want anything?"

"Nothing for him."

After a few minutes John returned with Wanda's drink.

"Thanks."

John excused himself and merged into the crowd as Colleen's husband sounded chimes.

"Ding..Ding..Ding...."

"Attention everyone. I would like to propose a toast to Colleen on her 60th birthday. May there be many more."

All raised their glasses.

John and the other Sullivan County attorneys gathered in conversation.

After finishing her drink, Wanda grabbed her husband,

"Bill, I'm not feeling well."

"I'll get the car and take you home."

"No, maybe it will pass. Let's stay."

Twenty minutes later she clutched her stomach and Bill whispered,

"That's it. Let's go."

Suddenly she bent over and fell on the ground.

Judge Henderson and several other guests quickly came over.

"Wanda, are you okay?"

"Oh, my God; the pain is horrible and it's getting worse. I need an ambulance!"

As Wanda was being carried out by the EMT'S who arrived within minutes, Judge Henderson surrepticiously looked at Sol with a sinister, knowing smile.

At the emergency room the ER Dr. Lui began the examination.

"It's probably the flu. To be sure, we'll conduct additional tests."

Wanda nodded in agreement as the nurse drew her blood then sent it to the lab.

As she laid in the ER she started to suffer pains in her chest.

"My God. Help me."

The heart monitor fluttered with irregularity; Wanda slipped into unconsciousness.

Code Blue was called and for the next 25 minutes the ER doctor and nurses furiously tried to revive Wanda. After an exhaustive effort Doctor Liu proclaimed,

"I'm sorry. We lost the patient."

Wanda was dead.

As Bill tried to sort through his confusion and make sense of what happened he spoke with the doctor,

"My wife just had a physical. The results were all positive. How could this happen?"

I am sorry, sir. May I strongly suggest that you have an autopsy performed."

Bill was reluctant but later conceded.

The next day the autopsy reported death from a heart attack.

Bill immediately contacted Wanda's primary care physician and advised him Wanda had passed away at the hospital.

"Were there any signs in her physical that indicated concern?"

"Absolutely not."

Bill called Ira and Colleen then gave them the bad news on Wanda's death from a heart attack.

Judge Henderson called Sol in New York.

"We just got the results on Wanda. She had a heart attack. Thank you for taking care of business."

"What are you talking about?"

"Didn't you take care of her?"

"No. There was no chance at your party. So she died naturally? I can't believe it. But it takes care of her and our problem."

They shared nervous laughter.

"Sol, are we going to get more cautious about the adoptions in the future?"

"Why?"

"The state is conducting an investigation into adoptions."

"Do you have any contacts in Albany?"

"Yes."

"I want you to check on this researcher named Rameriz. He's a dork and I just don't trust him. He is very nosey."

"Most researchers are that way but I will call my connections."

"We could also end up with the need for another personnel change, Sol. The problem is that almost every day Ira is pressed by Wanda and Rameriz and even the attorney John. And he's getting paranoid about the Liberty Police and worried about whether the investigation may be getting too close to him ... a real pain in the ass and a whistle blower risk to the whole strategy. Fewer people and cuts at some point in time would not be bad."

"Okay, Colleen. Not too soon though."

CHAPTER 100

—◆—

RAMERIZ TRIED TO CONTACT WANDA by phone but got no response. He proceeded to go to her home. As he approached he noticed a number of cars in the drive way and children playing on the side of the house. Rameriz knocked on the door and a strange woman answered.

"Is Wanda here?"

"I'm sorry, but Wanda passed away last night."

"You're kidding. What happened?"

"She had a heart attack."

"How old was she?"

"Sixty-three."

"Did she have any prior heart problems?"

"No, none that we were aware of. In fact she just had a physical and her doctor gave her a clean bill of health."

"Well I'll be dammed. Did they do an autopsy?"

"Yes, it confirmed the heart attack."

"Is her husband home?"

"Yes."

"I would like to speak with him."

"All right. May I have your name, please?"

"Oh, certainly. Rameriz."

"You can wait in the living room."

Rameriz sat on the couch and glanced around for Samantha's twins, who were not in sight. As the woman returned he asked,

"Where are the children?"

"They were moved to a temporary facility."

As Bill entered the living room, Rameriz stood and offered his hand.

"I am sorry for your loss."

"Thank you."

"When I met with her only a few days ago she seemed fine. I can't believe she is gone."

CHAPTER 101

—◆—

R AMERIZ DID NOT ASK ABOUT THE TWINS before he
left. When he got to his car he called John on the car
phone mounted on the console.

"John, have you heard about Wanda?"

"Yes."

"It's very strange."

"What do you mean?"

"It's just a feeling I have; nothing more.

"John, I wanted to tell you that we have decided to open
a formal investigation. We will make our intentions known.
I will tell Judge Hendersen that we are looking into the adoption practices of Sullivan County Family Court. I am setting
up a meeting with her and Ira, the social services program
director. We will also interview several adopton attorneys,
including Sol if he is available. If we can get the records we
will interview adoptive parents of some of the children and
the biological parents if available.

"I expect to meet with Judge Henderson in the morning
and notify her of our intentions."

"I am sure she will be delighted. You know how she just loves you, Rameriz."

They both chuckled.

At 9 a.m. the next morning Rameriz knocked on Judge Henderson's door.

"Come in."

Rameriz opened the door, walked towards her desk and laid a document on the judge's blotter.

"What is this?"

"Notification that we are opening a formal investigation into adoptions in Sullivan County."

"Tell me, how does a researcher convene a criminal investigation?"

"Well I am a bit more than a researcher."

He flashed his badge.

"I am Trooper Juan Rameriz, an undercover investigator for the state police. For the last year I have been investigating adoptions in Sullivan County. We are also investigating the role of the family court in the process."

"So you're not the egghead you act like. What do you want from us?"

"We will be conducting hearings starting within the next week or two. We plan to call a number of officials from the court and social services."

"Do you have a list?"

"I will be issuing subpoenas shortly."

"That is just fine with me. We have nothing to hide. Are there any other undercover agents in my court?"

Rameriz just smiled.

"We have a number of people in Social Services, including Ira, that we want to talk to about adoptions. We would like to talk to your friend Sol, but he seems to have disappeared. Do you know how I would contact him?"

"No. Maybe he went back to England to visit his mother."

"Let's leave that for another time."

Rameriz started to leave then stopped and turned to the judge.

"I think the people involved are close by."

"Really?"

"We are going to get to the bottom of this adoption scam."

"Well now; I'm glad to hear that. Maybe you will get a promotion if you solve the case."

Rameriz just smiled and walked out of the office.

Colleen immediately picked up the phone and called Ira.

"Rameriz was just here. He is an undercover investigator for the state police. They are going to start hearings pretty soon."

"So what. We are okay. Our asses are covered as you yourself always say, Colleen. You made me a believer, and now you're the worrier, aren't you."

"I'm going to call Sol and warn him."

"That's a good idea. I will talk to you at Wanda's wake at 3:00 p.m. today."

"Okay."

CHAPTER 102

———✦———

IRA HEADED TO AN AMERICAN BAR Association meeting being held in Peekskill NY after paying his respects at the wake.

As he listened to the radio a news story reported there were cracks in the wall along Route 6 / Route 202, commonly called 'The Goat Trail.'

"Crews will be performing construction activities, weather permitting, between the Bear Mountain Bridge and Annsville Circle. Motorists should expect delays and plan accordingly," DOT officials said.

Despite the news story and considering that the crews would not begin until the following day, Ira decided to take this opportunity to visit his girlfriend in Highland Falls, a short distance from the Bear Mountain Bridge which was just minutes diversion from his way back home.

As he was leaving for the meeting he looked at the weather report and saw there was a possibility that the long winding 'Goat Trail' drive could be difficult with the anticipated fog and heavy rain. As Ira proceeded his concern grew. Fog enveloped his car as he cautiously drove.

As the car climbed the mountain, Ira had to brake with each curve to attempt to control the car.

"Hmmm, I wonder if this was such a good idea."

As Ira approached the top of the mountain, he could not clearly see the white line markings and kept drifting into the oncoming traffic lane, then he would quickly turn back to his lane. With each swerve Ira lost control; he could not judge where the road started and ended. He started to call his wife on his car phone but reconsidered, knowing she would rag on him for going over The Bear Mountain Bridge instead of going the longer way via Route 84 through Newburgh. He would not want to disclose why he had persisted with the shorter route to see his girlfriend.

As he rounded the next curve Ira hit the brakes sharply and almost lost control of the car. As he slammed his foot on the brake it felt like he was touching the floor.

"It can't be. I just had the brakes inspected by my garage."

He changed to low gear to slow down.

As he reached the top of the mountain, conditions were very dangerous. He leaned forward, straining to see the road, his hands gripped the steering wheel so tightly his fingers were outlined on the leather steering cover. He felt sweat dripping down the front of his face and into his eyes and tried to find a place to pull over and wait for a break in the dense fog.

Ira was encouraged by the fact that oncoming cars were moving faster than he was, which gave some hope that the lower portion of the mountain was clearing. As he took the next curve he pumped the brakes out of habit and again noticed the pedal was close to the floor. He immediately and repeatedly pumped the brakes, desperate to gain control.

As he climbed towards the lookout point, Ira stepped on the gas to maintain speed and glanced in the rearview mirror at the lights from the car following him. A few seconds later Ira looked again and noticed the car was getting very close. He put on his flashers and braked … no response.

Ira's heart was pumping so strongly he could feel it through his shirt. Beads of sweat formed on his forehead. Just as he reached down for the emergency brake he felt a sudden thrust of his car moving forward. He looked into the rearview mirror at the car riding his back bumper pushing his speed to 80 miles per hour; a few seconds later his speedometer showed 90 mph; he picked up more speed against his will and hit 100 mph.

Ira gripped the steering wheel and continued straight, not able to see that, going East, The Goat Trail turns left just before the lookout. At that point, the car from behind rammed his car pushing it straight into the stone wall.

As Ira's car crashed into the wall, the supports cracked and the cement gave way. He tumbled down the steep cliffside.

Ira felt his wheels on the soil and stones; trees flew over the bumper. As he plunged over the cliff, he let go of the steering wheel, covered his face, grabbed his chest and slouched in the seat rolling over and over again.

At dawn the fog had cleared; the car lay upside down, badly mangled. Ira was crushed between the dash board and the roof of the car.

CHAPTER 103

———◆———

IRA'S WIFE CARRIE HAD BEEN UP all night expecting him to return. She had called his car phone with no response and wondered if he had stopped for a restroom or something. She called several times more with no answer. In utter desperation she called the State Police and reported her husband as missing. The police told her she must wait 72 hours before they began the search.

Carrie called Colleen. "Ira is missing!"

"What do you mean, missing?"

"He did not come home last night. He attended a Bar Association meeting and did not call me on the way home. That's not like him."

Colleen thought maybe it was more like Ira than his wife knew, considering his philandering, but said, "Is there anything I can do?"

"No, but thanks. I just wanted you to know."

"Call me later if you hear anything."

"Okay," said Carrie and hung up the phone.

A week later the state police received a call.

"Hello, I am George Heathcliff, a Boy Scouts leader. I took my troop on a field trip and while we were at The Goat Trail lookout, they saw a car turned upside down at the foot of the mountain, almost in The Hudson River."

After investigating the scene of the accident, the State Police identified the make and model of the car; a search of the body confirmed the identity -- Ira Tietz, Attorney at Law for Sullivan County Social Services, Monticello, New York.

They notified Ira's wife of the bad news.

Carrie called Colleen,

"Oh my God. Now I know where Ira was and why I didn't hear from him. He was killed in a car accident on the way to the Bar Association meeting."

Colleen was shocked.

"Did the police give you any details?"

"They had little information, but conditions on The Goat Trail were terrible that night; they suspect weather was the cause of the accident."

Colleen was devastated.

Later in the day Carrie again called Colleen.

"Someone reported to the police that they had seen a car slam into another car, but they had very few details and are doing an investigation. I'll call you when they tell me anything else."

A State Police investigator explained to Carrie that there was damage to the rear bumper, which also showed traces of paint.

"Was your husband ever in any other accidents?"

"No; he was a good driver."

"The damage to the rear bumper of your husband's car

cannot be positively determined as due to the fall or due to being hit by another car. However, we found chips of paint and matched it to a black BMW."

Carrie called Colleen and gave her the State Police information about the black BMW.

Judge Henderson was very upset and called Sol.

"I just got off the phone with Carrie. Ira's car was found. It is suspected that it was hit by a black BMW. I wonder if there is any connection to that nut who tried to run me over?"

"Colleen, it's got to be just coincidence."

Ira's wife Carrie inquired at Graceland Hospital if an autopsy would be conducted. The hospital explained it was not necessary unless she requested it.

"My husband was in good medical condition and he was a good driver, regardless of the weather. So I must do everything in my power to try and figure out what happened to him."

"We understand, Mrs. Tietz. It will take a few days before we have any results."

A week later the hospital advised her that Ira may have had a heart attack. Carrie called Colleen.

"I want you to know the findings from the hospital."

"What were they?"

"It appears the primary cause of death was a heart attack."

Colleen paused. "Carrie, did Ira have any heart problems?"

"None that I knew about."

Later that day, Carrie received a call from the State Police.

"Mrs. Tietz, did your husband have problems with the brakes on his car."

"No. Why?"

"It appears that Ira's brake linings were separated on the car."

"Could that have happened because of the crash?"

"It could have, but it's doubtful."

Carrie asked the investigator to keep her informed, hung up the phone and immediately called Colleen.

"The State Police just called me to ask about Ira's car."

"What about his car?"

"They wanted to know if he was having problems with his brakes. I told them he was not, but did Ira mention anything to you?"

"No. Why?"

"In going over Ira's car they found his brake linings were separated."

"Maybe it happened in the crash."

"No, the investigator said he didn't think so."

"Well, that *is* funny," said Colleen as she hung up the phone, and she called Sol.

"Did you take care of Ira as we discussed?"

"No, you just told me about the request. Don't you remember?"

"Yes, I remember."

"So, why do you ask?"

"The State Police are inquiring about the brake linings on Ira's car. Yet the autopsy showed he died of a heart attack."

"Hmmm. Let me know when his funeral is. I would like to attend."

"I don't think you should come, Sol. That undercover investigator Rameriz has been inquiring about you. I think you should lay low for now."

"Okay, Colleen. Keep me informed."

Carrie called Colleen.

"I was going through the contents in the car and discovered the garage statement showing that Ira just had the brakes fixed. I'm going to call Sherman's and see what they have to say."

"That's a good idea, Carrie."

Chapter 104

———◆———

AFTER THE FUNERAL, Rameriz obtained an interview with the judge. Judge Henderson looked across her desk at Rameriz with no expression and her answers were terse.

Rameriz questioned Wanda's substantial wealth. The judge screamed,

"How would I know?"

"What about Ira? What is his financial condition and net worth?"

"I don't go snooping into people's personal matters. And I certainly don't plan to investigate his assets now that he is dead."

"Don't you review their financial disclosures?"

"Yes, but I don't inquire how they acquired their money. Why don't you ask their spouses yourself? Did you investigate my financial disclosure?"

Rameriz did not answer.

"Well, did you?" screamed the judge.

Again, he failed to answer her challenge.

"Get out of my office!" yelled Colleen.

He turned, looked back and smiled.

"I'll be back."

Judge Henderson yelled louder,

"Get out!!!"

CHAPTER 105

———✦———

"I'M COMING TO NEW YORK FOR A VACATION," Judge Henderson announced to Sol in a phone call.

"Make sure we get together while you are in the City. There seems to be common denominator to all of these accidents. They all die from a heart attack without any previous history of disease."

"Yes, it is very strange how they are all dying suddenly."

"Is it an accident or is someone murdering these people?"

"Why? What would be their motivation?"

"How about revenge?"

"Revenge for what?"

"Maybe it's someone who didn't like the treatment they got from Social Services."

"How does that explain Wanda?"

"I don't know, Colleen."

The judge arrived at the Park Plaza Hotel and checked in at the front desk. As she was completing her information card, the desk clerk informed her,

"Judge Hendersen, we have a message for you," and

handed her a note saying

'Welcome to New York. I will see you later.'

Colleen smiled thinking it was from Sol. After she settled into her suite she called him.

"Hi Sol; I got your message."

"What message?"

"The one you left for me here at The Park Plaza."

"I didn't leave any message for you."

"Well, who the hell left the message?"

"I don't know."

"Sol, I am concerned that we are being stalked."

"By whom?"

"I don't know. I am going to call down to the front desk and see if it's a mistake."

"Call me later, Colleen."

"Okay."

"This is Judge Henderson. Can you tell me who left the message for me?"

"The message was delivered to the front desk clerk by a child. The envelope said: 'Please give this to Judge Henderson.' So it appears that there was no mistake. I am sorry, Your Honor. It probably was someone who knew you were in New York City."

At 7 p.m. Sol arrived at the hotel. He took a seat in the lobby and waited for Colleen to come down from her suite. After a few minutes she showed up and greeted Sol with a kiss on the cheek. "How are you doing, Sol?"

"I'm fine. Where would you like to eat? How about Tavern on the Green?"

"Okay. Let's catch a cab."

CHAPTER 106

———◆———

SOL AND COLLEEN WALKED BACK to the hotel after finishing dinner. As they crossed the avenue they both watched for traffic. Sol grabbed Colleen's hand and they both ran across the crosswalk.

As they attempted to cross the next avenue a black BMW with New Jersey plates went speeding by and turned on Fifth Avenue. Colleen motioned to Sol,

"Look – there's that BMW again. The windows are tinted so you can't see who's driving."

Suddenly the BMW came up the avenue and onto the sidewalk. Both Sol and Colleen ran into the door entrance to avoid being hit. They were shaken and Colleen's voice almost squeaked as she said to Sol,

"You see … somebody is trying to kill us. But who?"

Sol agreed, "This is no accident. Nobody comes up on to the sidewalk without a reason."

"While I am in New York, I want to hire you for protection."

"It's not needed."

"Bullshit. I'm not one to scare easily, but when the same

car runs me into the pond and comes up on the sidewalk of The Park Plaza, no less, I am afraid."

The next morning while Solomon and Colleen were having breakfast they heard a familiar voice.

"Hey judge, is that you?"

Colleen turned to see who was calling her.

"Rameriz, what are you doing here?"

He seemed to ignore the question and proceeded to introduce himself.

"So you're Sol. I thought you were in England."

"In England? Who said that?"

"Just a private joke…."

Colleen could barely hold back, then changed the subject.

"Do you know what happened? A black BMW tried to hit us when we were crossing the street."

"Are you sure?"

"Yes. The car went up on the sidewalk right towards us … he wanted to hit us."

"Maybe he just lost control."

"No way; this is the second time. The first time he followed me to the point I had to dive into the fountain pond in front of The Park Plaza Hotel. You are with the State Police; what should I do about it?"

"Did you get a plate number?"

"No; I was focusing on how to get away from him without getting hit."

"What kind of a car?"

"BMW."

"What color?"

"Black."

"There must be hundreds. But I will mention it to the city police."

"Thanks."

Rameriz nodded then asked,

"Sol, let's schedule an appointment to talk."

"Sure. Call me," and Sol gave Rameriz his card.

Chapter 107

⇥◆⇤

Sol and Colleen ate at their favorite lunch spot – Katz's Deli in the Bowery – again on Wednesday. As they were waiting for a cab to return they were not watching the traffic when a black BMW came up the avenue and suddenly veered directly toward them. Sol pushed Colleen out the way. She sat on the curb shaken. They quickly hailed a cab and said little on the ride back to the hotel. When they arrived, Colleen said in a dejected voice,

"Sol, that's it. I am going home in the morning."

"I will start investigating the incident, Colleen."

The next morning Colleen checked out early and left for Sullivan County.

Chapter 108

—◆—

RAMERIZ WAS BACK ON THE JOB. He contacted Anna.
"Where are the Jones twins' files stored?"

After a brief interude, Anna came back to the phone,

"I can't find the files."

"Who has the files?"

"I don't know."

Rameriz was frustrated,

"Anna, you may not be aware that you are impeding an investigation. Who was the attorney of record?"

"I don't know."

Rameriz was stumped. 'Why no records?'

He called John about the missing files.

"I suggest you contact the judge, Rameriz"

CHAPTER 109

———◆———

JUDGE COLLEEN WAS CALLED UP TO ALBANY to meet with the Chief Judge Tom Hyde. As she entered the building she saw Rameriz talking to him. When Rameriz saw Colleen coming he quickly excused himself and headed away from her down the corridor.

Colleen introduced herself and the two judges went into his chambers. At first, they engaged in small talk.

"What's new in Sullivan County?"

"Nothing."

They continued to converse until the chief judge said,

"Colleen, what are we doing to open the records for the past adoptions."

She made her case why the records should remain sealed. Despite her argument the chief judge cautioned her on not cooperating.

"It doesn't look good. It looks like you are hiding something."

"I am doing what I believe is right for the children and the adoptive parents."

"I don't agree with you, Colleen. I would think that you would be interested in getting this matter resolved. I will tell you that Rameriz is going to push this matter to the hilt."

"I don't care what Rameriz is doing or wants. I know what is best for me."

"Okay, Colleen. I will set up a hearing with a three-judge panel. It will take a week or two."

"That's fine," agreed Colleen.

As they were wrapping up there was a knock on the door.

"Come in," said Chief Judge Hyde, and Rameriz entered.

"Good morning. Nice to see you, Colleen."

She ignored the greeting.

"We are just finishing up, Rameriz."

"Do you want me to wait outside?"

"No, that's fine. Colleen was just leaving.

"I will call you later in the week," Chief Judge Hyde said to Judge Henderson.

After Colleen left the office Rameriz spoke with the chief judge,

"There is something wrong and she knows what is going on."

"Easy Rameriz; she is a judge and I don't want us to speculate."

"Okay."

Rameriz returned to his office in Albany and started reviewing the personal records of Colleen Henderson. According to her financial disclosure she had a moderate amount of assets for a judge. He then reviewed the personal records for Ira and Wanda. There was no unusual spending.

'If they are getting kickbacks; where is the money going? Offshore may be a possibility. How do I prove it?'

John called Rameriz.

"How is the investigation going?"

"We met in Albany last week with the chief judge. Judge Henderson is refusing to cooperate with unsealing the records. They have set up a three-panel judge to review the request."

"How do you think they will rule?"

"I think they will rule in our favor."

"I think about Samantha every day."

"Me too, John."

"I'll tell you, Rameriz, I want to see her children returned to her family. I want to see anyone involved in this scheme punished, especially if they are taking bribes."

CHAPTER 110

———◆———

J UDGE HENDERSON CALLED SOL in New York as she finished up her day.

"Have you found out anything that would give us a clue
as to who is behind this attempt to kill me."

"We still have no idea, but I have a number of people
working on getting us information."

"It makes me feel better that you are on top of this matter. Do you think Rameriz could be behind it?"

"I don't think so. What would be his motivation?"

"I just don't know. Anyway, I have to get going; I have a
meeting tonight."

"Okay; I'll talk to you later, Colleen."

As the judge entered the garage she looked all around
for any suspicious activity. She got into her car, pulled out and
headed for the meeting. She decided to use the back roads
instead of the highway. As she rounded the curve she spotted
a black BMW headed in her direction.

"Oh, shit...."

As it passed her she took a deep breath and continued to

drive, slower and with more caution. As she proceeded along the back road she noticed a number of cars were trailing her. After the cars passed, she put on the radio and settled down, able to relax.

Suddenly a car came right up behind her and started bumping the rear end of her vehicle. Colleen was shaken by the first bump; with the second she temporarily lost control as the car casually pulled out and passed her. She was able to recover control, then pulled off the road onto the shoulder and turned off the engine, stared at the car phone mounted on her console, and sat there waiting in the darkness with slight tremors in her hands as she grasped the steering wheel.

Colleen nervously looked in her rearview mirror … no cars were anywhere … nothing but darkness … silence.

She turned on the engine and pulled back onto the road.

Out of nowhere, a car came up, switched on their high beams and slammed into the back of Colleen's car. She swerved, bounced off the rocks then swung into the guard rail on the opposite side of the road. She was frantic.

'Why is this happening?'

She picked up the car phone … no service. She threw the receiver down on the floor and accelerated. A scenic view rest stop appeared like a desert oasis; she pulled in. Colleen got out of the car and inspected the damage … still driveable. She got back in, dug the key out of her purse, glanced out the window and there was the BMW barreling right towards her.

"Oh, Jesus God!!!"

The car struck Colleen's broadside with a harsh jolt, knocking her temporarily unconscious and shoving her car over and down the embankment.

Colleen came to slumped over the steering wheel with the entire right side of the car crushed and pinning her in. She could not move.

Suddenly she heard a voice,

"Are you okay?"

"I am badly hurt. I can't move. Please. Can you help me?"

"I have called the police and they are coming with the fire department now. Hang on. They will be here shortly," said the voice.

She saw a flashlight and yelled out,

"Over here. I'm in here!"

The flashlight beamed into the cracked window and she saw a familiar man peering in.

"Rameriz, is that you?"

"Yes, it's me all right."

"Thank God!"

Rameriz surveyed the damage,

"Colleen, we have to wait for the Fire Department. But there is no smoke."

Colleen heard sirens blaring in the distance as Rameriz asked,

"What happened?"

"A black BMW hit me broadside. I think he was trying to kill me."

"Why would you think that?" Rameriz baited.

"Jesus, Rameriz, is there anything under that curly black hair of yours? For God's sake, a fucking black BMW chased Sol and me off the sidewalk by Katz' then stalked us and we couldn't see who it was through the darkened car windows, like a hit man or something, and THEN on the very same day … oh, surprise, surprise … a black BMW ran me into the fountain by The Park Plaza and I walked in looking like a wet sewer rat … I get mysterious, threatening messages at The Park; now I'm sitting here after getting knocked out and my car broadsided and crushed by … hmmm, I wonder … oh yes, a black BMW … waiting for the fire truck … just in case my fucking car blows up while I can't move … what the hell is the matter with you … have you lost your marbles asking me why I think some asshole … always in a black BMW no less … is trying to kill me. Go figure … that's if you have figuring in your mentality. I don't know anything except you, Rameriz, are no longer one of the people I wondered might be trying to kill me … cause you don't happen to be driving a black BMW out here in the boon docks with the cute little deer and raccoons."

Colleen heard other voices in the background.

"The Fire Department is here," said Rameriz in a voice seemingly more sympathetic now that he succeeded in pushing the buttons of this judge who abused her power, stole children from their parents, and sold them to the highest bidder.

"Hold on; we will get you out."

The Fire Department cut the top of car off, pried out Colleen and placed her on a stretcher. Rameriz and three firemen slowly carried her up the hill to a waiting ambulance.

"I'll see you at the hospital, Colleen."

As the ambulance pulled away Rameriz went back to investigate the wrecked car. He managed to open the passenger door, pulled out some of the papers sitting in the glove compartment and picked up some that had scattered to the vehicle floor.

As he started to read and determine what they pertained to, the tow truck driver yelled at Rameriz, "GET OUT OF THE WAY!!"

He stuffed the papers into his jacket and climbed up the hill to his still-running car.

Rameriz drove to the local police office to report in.

"Gentlemen, I witnessed the BMW ramming the judge's car, pushing it over the bank. Then they just backed up and drove off."

"Is there any way it could have been an accident?"

"I doubt it. I tried to get the plate number but it was covered."

Chapter 111

————◆————

AFTER COMPLETING THE POLICE REPORT and further discussion, Rameriz excused himself, got on Route 17 by the little town of Hillburn and headed for Good Samaritan Hospital in Suffern. He pulled into the Security parking space and entered the emergency room.

Rameriz flashed his badge and asked to speak with the doctor.

"Hello. I am Doctor Hendrix. What can I do for you?"

"I am investigating the accident involving Judge Colleen Henderson? How is she?"

"She is in critical condition with internal injuries. At this point it's touch and go."

"Can I see her?"

"Only for a few minutes."

"Okay."

As Rameriz entered Intensive Care he could see the judge's face inside the oxygen tent and tubes in her nose and taped to her arms. Colleen was silent at first, then she raised her thumb, indicating she was cognizant and doing all right.

"I'll be back later to see you, Judge."

As Rameriz returned to his car he felt his jacket pocket and remembered the papers he had taken from the wrecked car. He put on the interior car light and started scanning. Suddenly he stopped reading and studied the West Indies Bank and Trust information: a deposit slip for the account of Colleen Henderson $55,000. There were three other slips: one made out to Ira Tietz's account for $25,000, one to Sol Bernstein for $10,000, and the last to Wanda Torres for $12,500. Rameriz quickly surmized that this might be the payoff for the Jones Twins.

The next morning Rameriz visited Intensive Care. He discussed with the nurse the critical nature of the injuries to Judge Henderson.

"How did she do last night?"

"We technically lost her three times."

"Can I see her?"

"Yes, but don't spend too much time questioning her. She is very fragle."

Rameriz entered Colleen's room. "How are you doing?"

Colleen raised her finger.

"Can I do anything for you?"

Colleen motioned for him and whispered:

"Get me a priest."

"I will."

Later that day Judge Henderson was visited by the chaplain who administered her last rites. He then went out to speak with the family.

Rameriz visited Judge Henderson a few days later. She was still in critical condition.

"Colleen, did you see the chaplain?"

"Yes," she whispered.

"I am glad you made peace with The Lord. Is there anything else you want to get off your conscience?"

"No."

"What about the adoptions of the Jones children? Where are they?"

Colleen shook her head; the plastic of the oxygen tent rustled.

"You know, Judge, you are not going to make it. Wouldn't you like to get this matter off your chest?"

Colleen paused then said again, "No."

"You're sure that what you did to the Jones twins will not have a lasting effect on your soul?"

Colleen started coughing and spitting out blood. Rameriz pushed the call button for a nurse and whispered,

"This is your last chance."

As the nurses attended to Colleen, he started walking out of the room.

"Rameriz, come back."

She told him where the children were and who the adoption attorney was in the case. Rameriz got Colleen to explain how the scheme worked and Ira and Wanda's involvement. He learned the location of the records that provided the names of the children, the adoptive parents, their addresses and how much money was collected. Rameriz quickly transcribed the information and had Colleen's confession signature notarized.

Throughout the confession, however, Judge Colleen Henderson completely denied any responsibility, or even involvement, in the deaths of Ira Tietz and Wanda Torres.

Rameriz contacted the chief judge in Albany and told him about Colleen's confession then placed her in protective custody, limiting any visitation of her to police only.

He left her with instructions to the police guard,

"There are to be no visitors without my consent. Even when someone from the police force comes, I must be notified and will be present."

Rameriz headed off to discuss the case with the district attorney.

CHAPTER 112

———◆———

J OHN NOTICED A NAME on the Patient Board when he was
visiting a friend … Colleen Henderson. He obtained her
room number and went to see her.

The police guard advised John,

"I'm sorry, sir. Judge Henderson may not have any
visitors."

Just as he was wondering what this was all about and leaving, Rameriz appeared and informed John of the confession.

"Wow, congratulations, Rameriz. Too little too late, but
at least this is an acknowledgment of the greed of that malev-
olent person who is in office to protect and serve, not abuse
and profit."

"I agree, John. Let's get together for lunch."

"Excellent. I've got to run; may I use the lavatory?"

"That would be all right."

John entered the bathroom, pulled out a pill bottle and
thought, "There's no better place than this; pill bottles are
all over the place." He threw it into the trash can which was
already full. It got hung up in the swinging top that stayed

partially open, which John did not notice. He washed his hands and came out.

"Thanks, Rameriz. See you soon."

The next time that day when Rameriz went into the bathroom, he washed his hands and disposed of the paper towel. As he shoved it down into the full can, he noticed the empty pill bottle.

'Hmmm, what's this?' he said.

He removed it, read the name 'Succinylcholine SUX' on the label and gingerly placed it in his jacket pocket. He took the pill bottle back to the station and ran it for fingerprints.

Rameriz called John,

"How about dinner tonight instead of waiting for lunch?"

"Sure. I'm free."

John and Rameriz talked about their days in the Marines.

"I was trained by the Navy and then assigned to a Marine Battalion."

"Why didn't you stay in the medical field, John?"

"After I was discharged from the Marines I worked at Beaufort SC Hospital. It wasn't quite right for me, so I decided to go to law school."

"So where were you stationed while you were in the Marines?"

"I was sent to the Philippines where I conducted a top secret research project investigating pharmaceuticals that could be used for creating heart attacks."

"That's interesting. How did you get into that line of work?"

"By accident, actually."

As they discussed John's background, Rameriz gathered that he had local contacts. John mentioned relatives in the Livingston Manor area, but he then quickly changed the subject.

"Are you married?"

"Yes. My wife was a nurse in South Carolina. One reason I decided to work here was for her to gain experience that would help her get a good job before we returned to South Carolina.

"How about you, Rameriz? Are you married?"

"No. One might say I'm married to my work, at least for this investigation."

They both enjoyed the meeting, but Rameriz was getting suspicious about John's background. The evening came to a close, and when Rameriz got home he came up with a reason that John would believe was valid for getting together again right away.

"Okay, John. See you for brunch at Stuffies."

In the meantime, Rameriz was able to get through to the chief judge who was hesitant to run a background check on John but agreed they had to uncover all stones to get to the bottom of the case.

First thing in the morning, Rameriz went to the Department of Veterans Affairs and determined that John had a Top Secret clearance, but what Rameriz was not ready for was that Samantha Jones' father was John's father.

'Really? ... Samantha was John's sister. How could that be? John said nothing about the relationship. Why didn't he disclose it?'

There were other details causing Rameriz to wonder if John even knew about the tie. The most significant fact was the research on heart attack drugs. John had extensive knowledge about the use of drugs to kill quietly and without discovery.

'Could John be the killer? Did he run the judge off the road?'

'Yet all of this evidence is circumstantial,' Rameriz concluded.

CHAPTER 113

———◆———

RAMERIZ TRIED TO DETERMINE IF JOHN was in the area at the time of the judge's accident. No, he was at an ABA meeting.

'That rules John out,' said Rameriz to himself … 'I am glad; I like that young man….'

At Stuffies, John showed up with another man and a woman and made the introductions.

"Rameriz, this is my stepbrother Marshall, and this is my wife Gabriella; we call her 'Gabby.' I hope it's all right if I brought them along. Marshall is here for a visit. I wanted you to meet my wife and him."

Breakfast was pleasant and friendly, but with the family there Rameriz could not ask the questions he needed to gather more information. They said their goodbyes and agreed to get together again.

The next day an important phone call came in from the hospital: Colleen had suffered a massive heart attact. Rameriz remembered what he saw on the pill bottle and quickly called the hospital advising of SUX.

The doctor at first dismissed the claim that Colleen could have been poisoned, but because of Rameriz's position of authority and persistence the doctor decided to test for the drug. Because the short elapse of time it was still possible to isolate the drug.

It was indeed SUX.

Rameriz learned that John was not present at the hospital and was relieved to rule him out as a suspect.

CHAPTER 114

———◆———

DURING THEIR BREAKFAST AT STUFFIES, Rameriz discovered that John's wife worked at the hospital. Since John was not present at the time of the attempted murder, could she be the killer?

The doctor administered an antidote in time to prevent Judge Colleen Henderson's death but the episode on top of the internal injuries from the car wreck meant recovery would take a long time.

The judge was transferred to Helen Hayes Reabilitation Hospital. Experienced in dealing with difficult patients or not, it was only a matter of time until the entire staff learned first hand how abusive she was. It was never possible to please her regardless of the effort.

An aide was assigned to the judge who did her best despite the constant harangue and demands.

CHAPTER 115

———◆———

COLLEEN HENDERSON WAS NOT an early riser, but the aide was committed to giving her a pleasant experience first thing in the day at least once.

"Good morning," was the lilting, singsong greeting by the aide as she drew open the drapes to darkness.

"Uuuuuuuuuuu."

"Time to wake up."

"Are you crazy? Not even a streak in the sky!"

"Come on, sunshine."

"There isn't any sunshine and I'm not sunshine. The only way I would be sunshine is if you had some valium in your pocket. I know I can have it; you just won't give it to me."

"Now, now. Let me get you ready. There is going to be a beautiful, beautiful morning. And you and I are going to go out and see it."

"Uuuuuu. Don't you ever get tired of being all make believe, bright and sparkly."

"No, no. Come on now, chicky. Let me brush your hair for you."

"You shouldn't get too close to me with that brush or *you* will be the chicky ... with a broken neck."

"Now, now. See ... your hair is still beautiful and curly. Everybody is going to see how lovely you look. Time to go. We don't want to miss the sunrise."

"Ok, ok. Anything to get you off my back."

The aide kept clucking as she wheeled the wizened judge out in the wheel chair.

"This morning the cafeteria is going to have your favorite Scottish tea. And we'll have a little milk in it with sugar."

"And you'll spill the tea in my lap while you talk with everybody."

"I'm not gonna do that. Be nice. Now, move your legs so we can get through the cafeteria door.

"'Hello, Joseph.' Look at these new doors, dearie ... they open right up for us. And the van is here waiting to go to Perkins Tower at the Bear Mountain State Park. It is a beautiful place where you can see for miles and miles and miles. It's wonderful."

Her gushing was met with hostile silence.

The aide carefully guided the wheelchair onto the van lift, climbed into the passenger seat and solicitously looked back to keep an eye on her ward to whom she was devoted despite the caustic personality. As they went North on Route 9W and wound through the wooded park, the judge, now older and even more caustic, did not hold back her sarcastic complaints.

Upon arrival, the aide pushed the wheelchair towards the lookout point.

"Oh, look at the neon pink peeping over the horizon. The sun is coming up. See, I told you it would be beautiful."

"You stupid selfish biddy. How could I see from here? Take me further so I can have a look. Don't you have any sense. Come on, get going!"

"Wow, it's really steep. We have to be careful now, dearie."

"Yeah, well, you're strong. Look at the arms on you. You look like a construction worker."

"I know, I know. Hmmm; I see a good tree on that flat rock. I can hang onto the branch and your wheelchair at the same time, so we'll be all right."

As the aide pushed the wheelchair towards the edge of the mountainside there was a sudden loud sharp clap … behind them … smoke spewed from the crevice. She snapped her head around, and saw a boulder starting to move, as though it were waking up. It was going to roll. She grabbed an overhanging branch and desperately tightened her other hand on the wheelchair. But it was too heavy; her ward, The Honorable Judge Colleen Henderson, slipped; the ground started to crumble and gave way.

"Help! Help! Help me you stupid bitch. You're letting me ……… Help! Help! Help!!!"

The aide began sobbing with the futility of her incapacity, a grimace on her face because she didn't save her ward. The only thing she could do was hold onto the branch for dear life.

As the wheelchair plunged off the edge of the cliff it tumbled over and over; legs flopped out; arms grasped for twigs, stones and the air; the chair rolled and smashed her bones against the rock outcropping; the boulders flew around banging and bruising; her screams for help were inhuman.

And then it was over.

There was nothing left but rubble.

But, no, there's a foot sticking out. And is that an arm? Is the finger on her hand moving or is that the smoke and dust rising like ashes?

"Waaaa. Waaaa." The screeching crescendoed as turkey vultures flocked above.

"Waaaa. Waa, waa, waaaaa!!!" Circling, circling and circling. Seeking the next meal.

Was that a whimper? A sob? A cry for forgiveness from our God in Heaven?

Justice Served.

www.ingramcontent.com/pod-product-compliance
Lightning Source LLC
Chambersburg PA
CBHW020235260626
47156CB00002B/685